"*Don't try to be smart!*"

"I can't help it—I *am* smart!"

"Not smart enough," Matt said grimly, "if you think that seducing me is about to win you a proposal of marriage."

"Win you?" Daisy yelled in disbelief. "You see yourself as some sort of prize, do you? Well, so do I—the booby prize!"

He glared right back at her and there was a silence while the only sound that could be heard was their angry breathing. And then he dropped his bombshell. "That's it!" he said decisively. "I'm going back to the States, Daisy!"

FROM HERE TO PATERNITY—romances that feature fantastic men who *eventually* make fabulous fathers. Some seek paternity, some have it thrust upon them—all will make it—whether they like it or not.

SHARON KENDRICK was born in West London, England, and has had heaps of jobs, including photography, nursing, driving an ambulance across the Australian desert and cooking her way around Europe in a converted double-decker bus! Without a doubt, writing is the best job she has ever had, and when she's not dreaming up new heroes (some of which are based on her doctor husband!) she likes cooking, reading, theater, listening to American West Coast music and talking to her two children, Celia and Patrick.

Books by Sharon Kendrick

HARLEQUIN PRESENTS
1820—PART-TIME FATHER
1867—MISTRESS MATERIAL

SHARON KENDRICK

His Baby!

Harlequin Books

TORONTO • NEW YORK • LONDON
AMSTERDAM • PARIS • SYDNEY • HAMBURG
STOCKHOLM • ATHENS • TOKYO • MILAN
MADRID • WARSAW • BUDAPEST • AUCKLAND

To my sister and brother-in-law—the learned
(and learning!) Tracey, and her gourmet
husband, Mick Maguire.

ISBN 0-373-11926-7

HIS BABY!

First North American Publication 1997.

Copyright © 1996 by Sharon Kendrick.

This edition published by arrangement with Harlequin Books S.A.

® and TM are trademarks of the publisher. Trademarks indicated with
® are registered in the United States Patent and Trademark Office, the
Canadian Trade Marks Office and in other countries.

Printed in U.S.A.

CHAPTER ONE

'WELL, that's that!' Mrs Hamilton put the phone back on the hook and smiled at Daisy. 'Matt's coming home for Christmas!'

Daisy had thought that the call might have been for *her*. Her mother was away, waiting for Daisy's sister to have her first baby. Never in her wildest dreams would she have thought that Matt was coming home.

But wasn't that what she'd wanted, been secretly hoping for—ever since Patti had died? That Matt would come home and make everything right in Daisy's world?

Matt.

Her heart pounded with excitement. 'He is?' she queried breathlessly, suppressing a great whoop of joy. 'Oh, but that's *wonderful*!'

Mrs Hamilton smiled. 'Isn't it?'

'How long for?'

'He didn't say exactly. But apparently he's going to be working in London for a few months before going back to the States. He wants to oversee a few property deals here.'

London? A ripple of excitement whispered its way down Daisy's spine. If Matt was working in London, then he would only be a couple of hours away by car—giving her *plenty* of opportunities to see lots of him, surely?

'He's bringing Sophie with him, of course,' continued Mrs Hamilton. 'So we'll need to get hold of a cot from somewhere.'

'And I haven't even bought them a Christmas present!' said Daisy in dismay. 'When is he arriving?'

'Tomorrow afternoon.'

'That soon?' But that was Matt for you—man of action.

'Mm,' said his mother. 'You know Matt; once he's made his mind up about something, he doesn't hang around. The flight from New York gets in to Heathrow mid-afternoon and he's arranged for a hire-car to meet him and then he'll drive straight here.'

'Did he sound very...upset?' asked Daisy tentatively, but Mrs Hamilton shook her head emphatically.

'No. That's the extraordinary thing; he didn't. He sounded just like Matt.'

So outwardly, at least, he wasn't playing the grieving widower, thought Daisy. But hadn't Matt always been a past master at keeping his feelings hidden beneath that devastating exterior? You never really knew what was going on behind those clever grey eyes or that coolly enigmatic smile. Daisy had once overheard one of his countless girlfriends complaining bitterly to him, 'You're nothing but a machine, Matt Hamilton—a beautiful, unfeeling machine!' And Daisy had jealously listened to his low, mocking laughter, his murmured reply, then silence, and had known that the 'unfeeling machine' was kissing his willing victim into submission.

'He must be feeling terrible,' said Daisy slowly. 'But I'd imagine he'd be very brave about it all; he always *was* brave, wasn't he? And it must have been the most awful thing in the world—his wife dying and leaving a tiny baby behind.'

Mrs Hamilton narrowed her fine grey eyes and gave a tiny frown. 'It must have been unspeakable. I just wish that he'd shared his grief with us, instead of staying on in New York with Sophie. But nothing changes the fact that I always thought that it was the most unexpected of marriages,' she said, with her familiar candour.

Daisy looked at her, open-mouthed, in amazement. 'You don't honestly believe *that*? What man wouldn't want to be married to a woman like Patti Page? International rock stars who look like top models aren't exactly ten-a-penny!' she added, unable to keep the trace of wistfulness out of her voice as she remembered Matt's stunning wife.

'For which we must be thankful,' said Mrs Hamilton drily, still smarting over the fact that her only son hadn't invited her to his wedding.

And then an awful thought occurred to Daisy. 'Mrs Hamilton,' she said slowly. 'You won't tell him, will you?'

'Tell him what?'

Daisy blushed. 'You know very well.'

'That you've foolishly chosen to leave school without taking any exams, thereby kissing goodbye to a promising career in mathematics? Is that what you don't want me to tell him, Daisy?'

Daisy's colour heightened even further. 'Er—yes,' she said, for once uncharacteristically hesitant. 'You know what Matt can be like.'

'I most certainly do. And, knowing Matt, I expect he'll find out whether you want him to or not.'

Daisy raised her rather square chin with determination, and her hair shimmered in a silky golden-brown curtain all the way down her back. 'Then we'll just have to make sure he doesn't find out. Now, shall I go and get his room ready for him?'

Mrs Hamilton smiled at her affectionately. 'Would you, dear? I think we'll put him in the blue room, shall we?'

The dreaded blue room. Daisy gritted her teeth as she remembered that dawn morning a year and a half ago, when she'd spotted a scantily clad Patti Page creeping out of the blue room where Matt had been sleeping, her hair all tousled—the look of a smug and satiated cat all over her face. Daisy might have been innocent, but you wouldn't have needed to be Einstein to know what she and Matt had been up to.

'Why not make up his old room?' she suggested quickly. Because surely it would only make his pain all the harder to bear if he was put in a room where he'd spent a night making passionate love with the woman he was later to marry? 'It might help him feel less miserable if he's in the room he had as a boy—surrounded by all those trophies he won at school and college.'

'*What* a good idea!' said Mrs Hamilton fondly, and the two smiled at one another in perfect accord, with the easy familiarity of two people who went back a long way.

Mrs Hamilton was almost like a second mother to Daisy. Daisy's mother and Matt's mother were the best of friends, had been at school together, had been bridesmaids at each other's wedding, then godmothers to their first-born—Matt and Daisy's elder sister, Poppy. So that when Daisy's father had run off to India to 'find himself', leaving behind a penniless wife with two children to support, Eliza Hamilton had offered her best friend what help she could.

Daisy's mother had become housekeeper to the immensely rich Hamiltons, though the only formality was in the title itself, and when Matt's father had died the two women had become even more like companions than employer and employee.

And Daisy had grown up alongside Matt. Ten years older than her, in Daisy's starry eyes Matt had been the expert on everything; he had taught her everything. It had been Matt who had shown her how to fly a kite; Matt who had discovered her outstanding talent for maths when he'd started teaching her chess. And Matt whom she had hero-worshipped ever since she could remember.

Daisy had fulfilled all Matt's predictions for her academic career. She had done outstandingly well at school. She had worked hard because she really wanted to shine—partly for herself, and partly to make Matt proud of her. But then one day he had run off and secretly married Patti Page, the world's most glamorous rock star, destroying all Daisy's secret dreams in the process. And after that nothing had ever seemed quite the same again...

But perhaps all that was about to change, she thought hopefully as she opened the door to his bedroom and gazed wistfully at all the trophies which dazzled in a silver line on the window-ledge which overlooked the paddock.

* * *

The hours before Matt was due home whizzed by faster than a big-dipper at the fairground, and Daisy and Mrs Hamilton rushed around the place like dervishes.

'Do you think this laurel garland is a bit over the top?' enquired Daisy as she leaned precariously over the oak bannister to fasten it so that it hung in fragrant green loops.

'A bit,' said Mrs Hamilton. 'But I expect he'll love it. He's been away too long—let's give him a really *English* Christmas.'

Daisy thought that she heard the sound of a car's tyres swishing to a halt on the gravelled drive, and she quickly ran downstairs to peep out of the window.

'He's here!' she said, her voice rising with the excitement which had been building up inside her all day. 'He's home!'

She watched as the sleek, dark car glided to a halt in front of the big old house. She was, she realised as her heart hammered away crazily, still an absolutely hopeless case where Matt Hamilton was concerned. Some things, she had discovered ruefully, simply never changed.

She peeped out from behind the heavy richness of the crimson velvet curtains into the gloom of the December afternoon, where the first white flakes of snow were beginning to fall from a pregnant, gun-metal-grey sky.

'What's he driving?' asked the car-mad Mrs Hamilton as she patted her hair in front of the mirror.

Daisy, who was completely useless where cars were concerned, screwed her eyes up so that she could just make out the silver badge which adorned the front of the vehicle. 'It's a Bentley, I think—a big, dark green Bentley. Very staid.' She remembered him driving home in the black, phallic Porsche which had so suited his effortless transformation from Cambridge scholar to hugely successful international financier. But Matt was a family man now... 'I'll go and open the door for him,' she said.

But by the time she reached the heavy oak door the old-fashioned bell was jangling imperiously, followed by a loud thumping which could not possibly be ignored, and she pulled the door open to the tall figure who stood like some dark, avenging highwayman amidst the cold flurry of snowflakes.

It was not how she had dreamed his homecoming would be.

Matt scarcely acknowledged her as he walked straight past her; he was too busy shielding the baby from the snowflakes which had started to come down in earnest. A bundle of thick white blanket was clasped against the shoulder of his black sweater and at that moment it gave a protesting little squawk.

'Hell! I've flown from one blizzard straight into another!' he exclaimed, then gave his aloof, rather enigmatic smile which nevertheless could melt the coldest heart. 'Hello, Mother.'

'Hello, darling.' Mrs Hamilton offered him her cheek.

And then the smoky grey eyes were turned in Daisy's direction. 'Hello, Daisy,' he said slowly, in the familiar, deep voice, but she thought that it

sounded harder, more cynical than she remembered, and his smile was strangely gritty.

'Hello, Matt,' she whispered.

The years had only increased the sheer physical
impact he made when he walked into a room. He
was tall and lean and rangy, and his eyes were the
colour of a stormy sea, his hair as black as a
moonless night. The angular slant of his high
cheekbones and the firm, jutting squareness of his
jaw made him look like some chivalrous Knight of
the Realm, who had strayed inadvertently into the
wrong century.

The bundle at his shoulder gave another protesting squawk, and his mouth underwent a dra-
matic and devastating transformation as it widened
into the tenderest smile Daisy had ever seen.

'And this is Sophie,' he said softly, loosening the
top blanket to reveal a chubby-looking baby of
about eight months. 'Little Miss Sophie Hamilton.
Say hello to Grandma and to Daisy, darling.'

'Hello, Sophie,' beamed Mrs Hamilton, and two
wide grey eyes looked around at her with interest.

The baby was the absolute image of her father,
Daisy realised as she stared into the smoke-coloured
eyes which were so like Matt's, and at the thatch
of dark hair which was already beginning to hint
at a recalcitrant wave. 'Oh, she's absolutely
beautiful!' exclaimed Daisy involuntarily, and Matt
looked down at her and gave her that swift, in-
dulgent look he had always reserved just for her,
and for a moment Daisy's heart stirred into ecstatic
life—as it had always stirred when Matt looked at
her like that.

'Isn't she?' he said quietly as the baby wrapped her tiny fist around his finger.

'Shall we take her into the drawing room?' asked Mrs Hamilton. 'It's much warmer in there.'

'And I'll make a tray of tea,' said Daisy, and shrugged when Matt looked at her questioningly. 'Mother's away—Poppy's baby is due any time now.'

'So Daisy's filling in for her,' put in Mrs Hamilton quickly. 'Doing all the cooking and housework until her mother comes back. Isn't that good of her?'

'That depends on whether your cooking has improved,' he said, giving a theatrical shudder, 'since you made me that disastrous birthday cake for my eighteenth.'

She remembered the chocolate-covered confection which had looked exactly like a cow-pat. 'Of course it has!' she answered indignantly.

He looked unconvinced. 'Well, I'm not risking it for Christmas lunch,' he drawled. 'Think you can book us a table somewhere, Daisy?'

'I can try.'

'Good. Oh, and Daisy?'

'Yes, Matt?'

'All this domesticity—it isn't affecting your schoolwork, I hope?'

'Of course it isn't!' she answered hurriedly, and she sped hastily off in the direction of the kitchen before he could read the damning lie in her eyes.

She slammed around putting scones onto a plate and adding hot water to the teapot, thinking that he had always been such a tyrant where she was concerned. Didn't he realise that she was no longer a child he could boss around? She was *eighteen*, for goodness' sake! Old enough to vote. To get married...

She added a milk jug to the tea-tray, mentally trying to justify to herself why she *had* left school so suddenly.

Part of the trouble had been that she had been a year older than the rest of her class-mates, thanks to a badly set broken leg which had had her in and out of hospital for the best part of a year. That year had isolated her, so that when she had eventually returned to school she'd felt an outsider. Added to which she'd been left with a slight limp in her left leg, which had only recently disappeared completely, and she had been badly teased about it for a long time.

In fact the limp had been a pain—in more than just the literal sense. Because it had altered everyone's attitude towards her. Her mother had fussed. Mrs Hamilton had fussed. Only Matt had refused to let the slight physical defect make any difference to his attitude towards her.

The scent of apple-logs filled the air as Daisy carried the tea-tray into the room. Mrs Hamilton had Sophie dangling on her lap over by the big bay window in which the Christmas tree glittered, and Matt immediately rose to his feet and took the tray from Daisy.

His grey eyes glinted as they looked her up and down assessingly and Daisy found herself, absurdly, *blushing*.

'Risking circulatory problems, aren't you, Daisy?' he said in a low murmur his mother couldn't hear.

It was a tone he would never normally have used with her, accompanied by a hostile look on his face that she wouldn't normally have seen there. Daisy stared at him uncomprehendingly. 'What are you talking about?'

His face was most *definitely* disapproving. 'Just that your jeans are so tight, I'm surprised you haven't cut off the blood supply to your feet altogether.'

Daisy bristled. They were new jeans, and she'd saved up for ages to buy them. She liked the way they hugged her small, high bottom and the way they clung lovingly to the long lines of her slender legs. And yes, OK, they *were* a little on the tight side—but that was the fashion—to wear them looking as though they'd been sprayed on. And the deep green sweater which picked out the unusual flecks in her golden eyes and which she wore tucked into the jeans—well, there was certainly nothing untoward *there*.

Of course Matt hadn't seen her for almost two years, and her body had developed rather alarmingly during that time. From being almost flat-chested, her breasts were now two rather lush and heavy curves which made her waist look far more slender than it had used to.

And unfortunately the newly curvaceous Daisy seemed to inspire most of the young men in the village to loudly whistle their appreciation at her every time she strolled down Cheriton High Street. Now, that she *didn't* like—but what was she supposed to do? Lock herself away in a nunnery?

She had let her hair grow, too, since she'd last seen Matt. Gone was the functional bob of yesteryear. Now it reached almost to her waist. Dead straight and lustrous, it was a rich golden-brown colour, thick as an armful of corn, and it spilled over her breasts like streams of satin.

She met a pair of mocking grey eyes. 'So you don't like what I'm wearing?' she challenged him.

'That isn't what I said,' he answered obliquely.

'And everyone's wearing this style at the moment,' she told him superciliously. 'Don't you know anything about fashion, Matt?'

'Enough,' he said curtly, 'to know that women who follow it so slavishly risk burying their individuality and end up looking rather like sheep.'

Mrs Hamilton, who had been busy clucking over Sophie, lifted her head and frowned as she heard the tail-end of the conversation. 'Sheep, did you say, Matt? What are you talking about? Daisy looks nothing *like* a sheep! Pour the tea, will you, darling?'

'Sure,' he said immediately, but there was a sardonic glint in his eyes as he handed a cup to Daisy and she had to fight very hard not to let the hurt and bewilderment show in her face, because this new and highly critical Matt seemed so *different*.

But why shouldn't he be different? she thought sadly as she sipped at her tea. Why shouldn't he be cold and hard and aggressive? He had been married and widowed within the year, left with a baby daughter to look after. His wife's funeral had been just over a month after the birth of their child, and grief did strange things to people.

He leaned back in his chair and drank his tea, tall and dark and very faintly forbidding. He looked remote—a glamorous, stylish stranger. It was hard to believe that this was the same Matt who'd taught her to ride, told her which books to read, described the world he'd seen in all his travels. Matt whom she had adored and worshipped for just as long as she could remember.

She had been only eight when he had gone up to Cambridge, but she could still remember how bitterly she had cried that first night after his departure. Nothing, she had thought, would ever be the same with Matt gone. And how right she had been—for nothing *had* ever been the same with Matt gone.

Daisy had been unable to repress that painful jealousy she'd felt whenever he had come home in the college vacations, usually with some bright, smiling golden girl clinging onto his arm, though she'd taken great care not to show him how she felt.

And now, as she covertly watched those long, lean legs which seemed to stretch endlessly in front of him, Daisy wondered how on earth she had ever had the temerity to imagine that someone as gorgeous as Matt Hamilton would ever be remotely interested in someone like *her*.

He finished his tea and when he'd put the cup down he rose elegantly to his feet. 'Shall I hold Sophie for you while you drink your tea, Mother?' he said, and at the sound of his voice the baby turned and gurgled, dropping her fluffy pink bear on the carpet as she virtually launched herself out of his mother's arms and into his, and he smiled, his hard face relaxing again as the baby joyfully settled herself into her father's embrace.

Daisy stooped to pick up the bear Sophie had dropped, and when she straightened up it was to find Matt staring at her again, an almost imperceptible disquiet shadowing the narrowed grey eyes.

Mrs Hamilton was looking from one to the other of them with an expression very like bemusement, and she shook her head slightly as she stood up. 'I have to ring Harry down in the village to check what time he'll be delivering the champagne for Christmas morning. Don't forget that the hordes will be arriving for drinks, will you, darling?' she asked her son.

Matt pulled a face and Sophie giggled. 'Will I be allowed to forget?' he murmured.

'No, you won't,' answered Mrs Hamilton firmly as she breezed out of the room. 'It's a family tradition!'

Matt scooped Sophie further up his chest, so that she was looking with perky interest over his shoulder, and then he indicated a hold-all he'd brought in. 'Would you mind unpacking that bag for me, please, Daisy?'

'Of course I wouldn't mind!' Pleased to have something to do other than try not to keep staring at that peculiarly disapproving face, Daisy crouched down on the floor to unzip the bag, taking out cotton-wool balls and lotion and all the other mysterious baby paraphernalia which lay inside. She could sense that he was still watching her, and it made her conscious as never before of the blue denim clinging to her bottom.

There was an odd kind of silence in the room, which even Sophie's occasional glug couldn't dispel. Daisy could feel more of that self-conscious colour stealing into her cheeks and the increased thud of her heart as she acknowledged the unique tingle of self-awareness which Matt seemed to have bestowed on her like an electric charge. Rather desperately she hunted around for something neutral to say.

'Somehow I can't really imagine *you* changing a nappy, Matt!' she commented, but she saw the sardonic twist of his mouth and knew that she had not succeeded in lightening the mood at all.

'Why ever not?' he queried, in a mocking drawl. 'These are the nineties, after all, and fathers are hands-on these days. Or did you imagine that rich, successful tycoons don't behave like other fathers?'

There was something so cynical about the way he spoke that Daisy sat back on her heels and looked up at him in bewilderment, wondering what had happened to make his grey eyes shine with that brilliance which was as cold and as hard as a diamond. Was that what bereavement did to you?

'I—didn't mean anything like that,' she said in confusion. 'I don't know any fathers of your age, for one thing. And for another you're not some "rich, successful tycoon", as you put it—you're just Matt to me. The same Matt you always were.' Which sounded so naïve that she bit her lip as she said it, wishing that she'd learnt to think before opening her mouth.

But Matt smiled then, and his real smile, too— not some pale masquerade of the real thing. 'Of course you didn't mean it. Take no notice of me, Daisy. I'm tired and I'm jet-lagged and Sophie's teething—'

'And you're still not over Patti?' she prompted gently, praying that he might confide in her. She might have once felt jealous of the woman who had captured Matt's heart, but Patti was now dead, and Daisy would have done anything to be able to take that bleak, haunted look from his eyes. 'Oh, Matt—it must have been absolutely awful—I kept thinking about you. That letter I wrote was painfully inadequate.'

He shook his head. 'No. Your letter meant a lot to me.'

'I wanted to come to the funeral, and I know that your mother did too—but since it was being held in New York and you didn't really seem that keen . . .' Her words tailed off because she could see the sudden, warning tension in his body.

His mouth tautened as though she'd said something obscene, and Daisy was shocked by the expression which hardened those beautifully angular features. 'Daisy . . .' He seemed to be choosing his words carefully. 'I know that you mean well, but I have to tell you that I don't want or intend to discuss Patti with you. Dwelling on her death will not help anyone, and certainly not Sophie. I have a new life to make for myself, and I have to let go of the past. Do I make myself clear?'

'Perfectly,' said Daisy stiffly, and for a moment she felt a fleeting pang of sympathy for his dead wife. Who would ever have dreamed that Matt could be such a cold fish as to dismiss the woman he had married as though she were some troublesome item on an agenda Daisy had been proposing?

What was more, he'd never spoken to her like that before. Never. Not in that curt, abrupt, dismissive manner.

Inevitably Daisy's mind drifted back, took her to the last time she'd seen Matt Hamilton, eighteen months ago, before his life was to alter irrevocably...

He was due back from the States for a short holiday and his mother had decided to throw a summer ball in his honour at Hamilton House. Since he'd gone to live in New York after graduating his visits had been few and far between and they'd all missed him terribly, Daisy especially.

She was over the moon with excitement. Her first ball, and, much more importantly, Matt was to be there...

She was in a real panic about what to wear, and eventually her mother sewed her a dress, made from an old ballgown of her own. Her first really grown-up dress.

Daisy twirled around in front of the mirror, admiring the pale blue gauzy voile of the skirt which floated over a stiffened petticoat down to her slim ankles. The bodice of the dress was in the same silvery blue, but made of satin, and it was strapless and clung to the faint swell of her burgeoning breasts. It wasn't a particularly fashionable dress, but she loved it.

The strappy silver sandals were borrowed from a schoolfriend and her hair swung neatly to her small chin in a glossy bob, two boot-lace strands of silver ribbon catching it up at the sides so that it didn't fall all over her face. She wore a lick of mascara which emphasised the dark lashes which framed her hazel eyes, and a brush of gloss on her lips. For a girl who had never dressed up she felt like Cinderella as she waited for Matt to arrive.

But Matt was late; he phoned from the airport to say that his flight was delayed, and Daisy, who'd been hovering by the door waiting for him, took the call, her heart plummeting with disappointment when she heard his words.

'I'll try and be there by ten,' he promised.

She looked up at the grandfather clock in the hall, biting her lip as she did so. Ten! But that was nearly two *hours* away!

She tried to make the time go faster. She ate some salmon and then some strawberries and cream which she didn't really want. She drank one glass of champagne, danced with all kinds of young men she had no desire to dance with, and all the time her gaze darted anxiously to the door, just waiting for the moment when Matt would appear, and he would see her and...

Well, she wasn't sure *what* would happen then, because in her innocently youthful fantasies she had never got beyond that particular moment when his eyes would light up with delighted fascination as he saw just how much she'd grown up...

As it happened, he arrived without her seeing him. She was at the far end of the room when she heard a split second's silence, followed by a buzz of excitement, and Daisy turned around to see the tall, elegant figure in a superbly cut dinner jacket which emphasised the breadth of his shoulders, the light from the chandeliers setting the ruffled dark hair gleaming.

He must have sensed that someone was staring at him, because the brilliant grey eyes sought her

out immediately, and they narrowed for a moment
with an appreciative yet frowning intensity which
for some reason made her skin come out in goose-
bumps. She honestly thought that she might run
the full length of the room and into his arms when
something stopped her.

He wasn't alone.

By his side stood the most beautiful woman she
had ever seen. She looked astonishingly and disturbingly familiar, thought Daisy, frowning as she
tried to think of when or where she'd seen her
before.

The woman had a riot of shiny blue-black curls
snaking exotically all the way down her back, and
eyes which were greener than an avocado. Her unbelievably tiny-hipped body was clothed in a long,
tight sheath of emerald sequins, so that she resembled some fresh and slim blade of grass. The
dress was completely backless and slit on both sides
right up to the woman's thighs, leaving no one in
the ballroom in any doubt that she had the most
superb body that most men would ever see in a
lifetime.

Daisy heard a shocked choke from behind her as
one of the guests almost spat his champagne out
to exclaim, 'Good grief! Trust Matt Hamilton to
have all the blasted luck! That's Patti Page with
him, isn't it?'

Daisy stared even more and so did everyone else
in the room, drawn to that startling, exotic beauty
like moths to a light bulb. No wonder the woman
had looked so familiar, but also no wonder Daisy
had failed to recognise her. Because you didn't

expect to see a world-famous rock singer attending what was simply a provincial summer ball!

Matt began to move forward, introducing the beauty on his arm to all and sundry, and Daisy turned away and stumbled out onto the moonlit terrace, knowing that the overwhelming disappointment she felt was totally unreasonable, but unable to shake it off all the same.

He was *twenty-seven*, for heaven's sake, and she was seventeen. He lived and worked in New York, and she was at the local school. He was a sophisticated, successful man of the world who had always had legions of women clamouring for his attention, and she had never even had a single boyfriend. So what had she been expecting? That Matt would take one look at her in her finery tonight and then tell her dramatically that he would wait for her, for just as long as it took?

'Hello, Daisy,' came a deep, familiar voice, and Daisy whirled round to stare longingly up at that magnificent face.

'H-hello, Matt,' she stumbled.

'You're looking very beautiful tonight,' he said gravely as the grey eyes slowly looked her up and down. 'Although I expect that a lot of people have already told you that.'

No one else who mattered, she thought. 'Wh-where's—your girlfriend?' she managed, and in all the best fantasies Matt would have said, with a frown, 'My girlfriend? Oh, Patti's not my *girlfriend*—she's going out with my best friend/colleague/the man I met on the plane...'

The trouble was that he didn't say any of those things. 'Patti?' He smiled, and Daisy was old enough to recognise the speculative sexual glint which came into his eyes. He's sleeping with her, she recognised, with a pain that kicked her in the stomach with the force of a sledgehammer.

'Oh, Patti's gone to repair her make-up. That generally takes something in the region of half an hour, so I just thought I'd come and steal a dance with you while I was waiting.'

He didn't even give her a chance to say no, although afterwards she wished he had. Because one moment in Matt's arms was enough to give her a taste of a forbidden paradise, and she knew that she would never be quite the same again.

Just for that one dance, Daisy closed her eyes and let herself go, drifting with him in time to the music and letting her feelings guide her rather than her judgement. She melted into his embrace, entwined her arms around his neck as though it was the most natural thing in the world. And she found that her body was drawn so sinuously close to his that it was difficult for her to breathe.

She could feel him stiffen with a sudden tension, and she was tightening her arms ecstatically around his neck when she heard him say, very abruptly, 'Easy, Daisy. Easy,' he repeated, frowning, a glimmer of surprise and remonstration in his voice as he loosened his hands, which had been holding her waist. And then the spell was broken.

'Matt?' It was a drawled, sexy American accent, and Matt and Daisy drew apart to find the green goddess standing next to them, scrutinising them with those magnificent avocado eyes. 'My, my, Matt,' came her acidly amused comment. 'What's this—cradle-snatching? She's just a little young for you, isn't she, honey?'

Matt laughed easily and let Daisy go, taking hold of the American woman's strong, slim hand and lifting it briefly to his mouth. The gesture stabbed at Daisy's heart like a stiletto. 'This is Daisy,' he smiled, 'whom I've known since she was a little girl—she's my honorary sister, aren't you, Daisy?'

Daisy tried not to grit her teeth with frustrated rage as she nodded obediently.

'And I'd like you to meet Patti Page,' said Matt.

'H-hello,' stammered Daisy, feeling as flat as she always did the day after her birthday.

'Hi,' said Patti, her superb lips twisting with barely feigned amusement as she took in Daisy's very obviously home-made dress. 'Honey,' she purred into Matt's ear, 'I'm absolutely starving. Something or *someone's* given me the *biggest* appetite.' And here she winked suggestively at Daisy. 'So can we please go *eat* something?'

'Of course we can,' he answered, and Daisy saw the American woman's hand slide possessively underneath his jacket, could see it moving sensuously beneath the soft, dark cloth in a gesture which just shrieked of sexual possessiveness, and Daisy knew a very real desire to scream out loud.

'I'll see you later, Daisy,' Matt told her.

But she didn't see him later, not to talk to, though she found him watching her across the ballroom from time to time, that curiously intense look on his face again. All Daisy saw was Patti creeping out of his room at dawn, and the following morning they both drove off very early, and at great speed.

And within weeks came the news that Matt and Patti were married and were expecting a baby...

Slowly and reluctantly, Daisy came back to the present to find Matt watching her, his elegant dark brows quizzically raised.

'Such pensive daydreams, Daisy,' he mocked softly, in a knowing voice. 'Care to share them?'

Had he guessed? Could he tell by her face that she'd been thinking about him? Was she really so transparent—or was it just that Matt was uncannily perceptive where she was concerned?

Daisy pushed a wayward strand of hair out of her eyes and rose to her feet. She had to get out of here. Matt's presence had awakened too many confused feelings within her. 'Please excuse me,' she said politely. 'I want to go and wash my hair.'

'Oh?' came the arrogant query. 'It looks fine to me.'

'Not fine enough,' she corrected him stiffly, and then, as if to prove to him that she was no longer a child, she added, 'I'm going to a dance tonight.'

'A dance?' Daisy might have been suggesting a solo space mission, from the look on his face.

'Yes, a dance!' she retorted. 'Don't sound so surprised, Matt. This may not be New York, but we have quite an active social life here in Cheriton.'

'Do you really?' he murmured, and Daisy got the distinctly annoying feeling that he was laughing at her.

CHAPTER TWO

ALONE, in the sanctuary of her bedroom, Daisy piled her newly washed hair on top of her head. Did *that* make her look more sophisticated? She peered at herself critically in the mirror. Not really. Sighing, she reluctantly pulled the pins out and the golden-brown hair spilled in satin tendrils over her breasts.

Which meant that it was going to take what she *wore* to convince Matt Hamilton that she was not some wayward little schoolgirl he could patronise like mad, but a living, breathing *adult*!

Her wardrobe wasn't exactly extensive but she had something to suit most occasions, and one dress in particular which would score very high in the razzle-dazzle stakes. Black and slinky, it was the most outrageous garment she possessed. She slithered into it and surveyed herself in the bedroom mirror again. Perfect! Absolutely perfect!

In black Lycra, it clung like a second skin and skimmed to midway down her thighs. She wore it with opaque black tights and understated black pumps and then completely went to town on her make-up. When she'd finished she was satisfied; the glitter of green shadow emphasised the flecks in her golden eyes and the rose lip-gloss the full curve of her mouth. Her hair she left falling unfettered, so that it swung in a scented golden-brown curtain all the way down her back.

The only vaguely festive jewellery she owned was some glittery stuff which had been fashionable last year, and she clamped on the big, dangly earrings and the matching bracelet, and was just coming out of her bedroom when she almost collided with Matt coming out of his.

He had obviously just been putting Sophie to bed, since he had removed his black cashmere sweater and there were damp patches spattered all over the front of his grey shirt. Evidence of a playful bathtime, she thought with a sudden wistfulness, wishing that he'd asked her to help him.

His mouth curved into a disdainful imitation of a smile as his eyes slowly flicked over her with all the judgemental deliberation of a sergeant major inspecting the troops.

'Well, what do you know?' he murmured sardonically. 'Here we have another illustration of Daisy's sartorial elegance. And this time we find that the fairy has fallen off the top of the Christmas tree and landed right here in front of me.'

She kept the smile pinned to her lips. 'And if that's supposed to puncture my confidence,' she told him sweetly, 'then I'm afraid you haven't succeeded, Matt. Better luck next time!'

He ignored her remark. 'So where are you really heading tonight, Daisy? To some tacky strip-joint where you're the star turn?'

'And you can keep your cheap comments to yourself!' she snapped back at him, furious as a cat who'd been confronted by water. 'You obviously know absolutely *nothing* about women and what we like to wear.'

He gave a cool smile, and a spark of challenge
lit the bright grey eyes. 'You don't think so?' he
murmured. 'Well, I'm afraid that I'm going to have
to disabuse you of that opinion, my dear Daisy. I
happen to know enough about women to advise
you that if you have it, then it's definitely best not
to flaunt it. Unless you're aiming for the trampy
look.'

A slow flame of anger began to build inside her,
and all the pent-up hurt she'd felt when he'd gone
off and married Patti came bubbling to the surface.
'But Patti flaunted it, didn't she?' she taunted
recklessly as she remembered that backless dress
with the slits all the way up the side which had revealed her magnificent body. And then she stopped,
appalled at herself as she realised what she'd said.
'Oh, Matt,' she began remorsefully. 'I'm so sorry.
I didn't mean it—'

His mouth was a hard line as he moved a little
closer. 'But you did mean it,' he contradicted her,
in a voice soft with menace. 'You know you did,
Daisy.'

Suddenly, this was no longer the Matt she knew
and remembered—the combination of protector
and childhood hero. This Matt was altogether more
threatening—dark and brooding and exuding
something, some indefinable something, which sent
a shiver of excited recognition all the way down
Daisy's spine. She bit her lip, feeling way, way out
of her depth. 'I shouldn't have spoken ill—'

'Of the dead?' he put in.

'Yes,' she whispered. 'I'm sorry.'

He shook his head. 'But it's the truth, Daisy, and
we're taught to speak the truth. Patti *did* flaunt

herself. She was beautiful, and she knew it. Her career as a singer capitalised on the flaunting of that beauty. But you're no rock singer,' he finished, and his eyes hardened. 'And what you're wearing I would have thought was a little unsuitable for a hop at Cheriton Village Hall. I don't quite think the locals are ready for it, do you?'

He gave his old, familiar smile then, and Daisy recognised the gesture immediately. Matt *thought* that he was about to get his own way and so he was laying on the charm with a trowel.

Well, he darned well *wasn't* going to get his own way, not this time! Daisy pursed her lips together indignantly. 'And what gives you the right to come back here and start dictating what I should or shouldn't be wearing?'

'Right?' He looked genuinely perplexed, the harshness having momentarily fled from his face. 'Why, the right of friendship, of course. I thought we were friends—and friends look out for one another, don't they?'

Daisy stared at him and felt a sudden sadness overwhelm her. Friends?

No.

She and Matt were no longer friends. Something had happened to friendship along the way, and it had become something far less innocent... Somewhere along the way, her girlish crush had matured into a tugging pull of desire. Her innocent fantasies had blossomed into real needs. Because when she looked at Matt now it was with the acknowledgement of his potent sex appeal, the earthy charisma which he exuded like an aura around him. She found herself wondering what it would be like not just to kiss him but to lie naked beside him, to have all that virile strength embracing her...enfolding her...

She shivered slightly and pushed the disturbingly erotic thoughts away as she met his steady gaze squarely. 'And now, if you've finished your little lecture, please may I be excused?'

'Be my guest.' He gave her a humourless smile. 'And how do you propose getting to this—er—dance?'

'I'm getting a lift, actually.'

'A lift?'

He made it sound as though an alien spacecraft was about to land on the lawn outside. 'Yes, a lift. *You* remember, Matt. Car draws up to house. Driver gets out, opens door. Daisy gets in. Car goes "broom-broom!" and roars off at speed!'

'Don't be so damned flippant!' he snapped.

'Then don't be so damned autocratic!' she retorted, with a shake of her head which set her hair shimmering, ridiculously pleased as she saw him watch the movement with reluctant fascination.

'And just who's giving you this lift?' he enquired silkily.

Daisy opened her mouth to reply, but at that precise moment the doorbell clanged. 'See for yourself,' she told him sweetly, and ran downstairs.

'Oh, I shall,' he said softly, from just behind her.

Daisy had been rather pleased when Mick Farlow had invited *her* to the village dance, since he happened to be flavour of the month. And no wonder. At a towering twenty-one years old, with a thatch of thick blond hair and the kind of shoulders which could support at least two women sitting on them,

Mick was the local dreamboat. Even Daisy had agreed that. But that had been before she'd known that Matt was coming home...

So perhaps it wasn't surprising that as Matt unsmilingly opened the door to her would-be suitor Mick Farlow should suddenly pale into complete and utter insignificance beside the tall, dark man who seemed to dominate the spacious hallway. It was like comparing a candle's light to a flaming beacon.

Daisy thought how boyish Mick looked compared to Matt. How smooth and shiny his skin was, when contrasted with Matt's virile and shadowed jaw. He even looked ill-at-ease in his best suit, the tie sitting awkwardly on his broad neck. Matt, who was casually dressed in black jeans and a grey shirt, somehow managed to look more elegant than Mick in all his formal clothes. All of a sudden, Daisy heartily wished that she weren't going to the dance.

'You've come to collect Daisy, I believe?' asked Matt.

'Er, that's right—sir.'

Daisy closed her eyes in despair. *Sir?* Oh, for heaven's sake—now Mick was sounding positively feudal!

'You'll not be drinking, I hope?' And it sounded more like an order than a question, thought Daisy indignantly. Of *course* he wouldn't be drinking.

'N-no, sir.'

'And what time do you propose having her home?'

At this point, Daisy thought, she would explode with rage. He was acting like some sort of jailer,

for heaven's sake! 'Go and get in the car, Mick,'
she instructed. 'I'll be out in a moment.'

'But—'

'*Now!*' she ordered firmly as she gave him a
gentle shove out of the door, before turning to stare
indignantly up at Matt.

'Do you think that you can suddenly arrive back
here and start playing the heavy?' she demanded
furiously. 'Or does it just do your ego good to have
Mick kowtowing to you as if you were the village
squire?'

The grey eyes glittered. 'I really don't see what
you're so uptight about, Daisy. I would have
thought it was perfectly normal to enquire when we
might expect you home. It's a question I would have
asked if it had been my mother he was driving. The
roads are particularly icy at this time of year, as
I'm sure you know.'

Oh, how great to be compared to his mother!
'Mick's a perfectly good driver!' defended Daisy,
who had never been in a car with him in her life.

'I'm delighted to hear it,' answered Matt ur-
banely, but his eyes were hard as they flicked intently and tellingly at the amount of leg she was
showing. 'And is that all he's good at, I wonder?'

Daisy's cheeks flamed at the implication and at
the sudden fizzing of excitement which his cool
scrutiny of her legs could provoke. 'That was a
cheap remark!'

He shrugged. 'Only if you choose to interpret it
that way. I could have been talking about his ability
to handle a—tractor.'

'Oh, sure!'

'And you still haven't told me what time you'll be home.'

'The dance finishes at eleven,' said Daisy reluctantly, because she knew that determined glint in Matt's eyes of old.

'Good. I'll expect you back by eleven-thirty. I'll wait up,' he added, his eyes glittering with a spark of humour as he registered the set line of her mouth.

Something about his confident self-assurance and that arrogant grace sent her blood-pressure soaring. 'You've been away for years!' Daisy, who knew it down to practically the very second, cried exasperatedly. 'So how do you think I've managed to survive without your bully-boy tactics up until now?'

There was something very like a warning glint in those narrow grey eyes. 'I don't know, Daisy,' he murmured softly. 'But I intend finding out. You certainly aren't the same girl I remember.'

'Of *course* I'm not! I'm eighteen years old now!'

'Positively ancient,' he mocked.

'And I'm not a girl any more—I'm a...' She flushed but still stared at him defiantly, just daring him to make fun of her. 'Woman,' she finished, but reluctantly.

The blazing grey gaze was very steady, no trace of mockery there now. 'So you are,' he said quietly, and then, on a different, indefinable note which made Daisy's heart lurch, he added, 'Somehow I wasn't expecting it. And now I must go and check on Sophie. Goodnight, Daisy.' But just before he turned to walk up the stairs he gave her a long, hard look, and she remembered just how for-

midable he could be. 'And don't be late,' he added
softly.

Daisy gulped as she watched his dark, retreating
frame, her eyes unwillingly drawn to the long, long
legs in the black denim, the broad shoulders in the
soft grey shirt. Don't be late! She'd be as late as
she liked! She certainly wasn't afraid of Matt.

She wasn't!

Well, maybe she was. Just a little bit. And wasn't
it best to humour him? Because there was no way
she wanted him to discover that she'd opted out of
doing her exams and didn't have a *clue* what she
wanted to do in the future. Daisy shuddered as she
tried to imagine Matt's reaction to *that*. No way.
She couldn't face his anger—certainly not at
Christmas.

But there was no reason why he *should* find out,
she told herself reassuringly as she pulled on her
thick black coat and buttoned it up to her neck.
Mrs Hamilton had promised faithfully that she
wouldn't breathe a word to Matt. And she wouldn't
go back on a promise. And, she thought, if he *was*
only here for a short while, he'd be busy with the
baby and catching up with his old friends for most
of the time.

Especially friends of the female variety, thought
Daisy gloomily. No doubt every woman within
miles would soon be flocking to the house, like ants
crawling over a jam-pot, once news got round that
he was back. There was something very appealing
and romantic about a man looking after a baby
on his own at the very best of times, but if that
man happened to possess over six feet of dark,
devastating charm, with a mind like a steel trap,

and a self-made fortune which would rival Rockefeller's—then he'd probably have to fight them off in droves.

Daisy was filled with a stubbornly persistent air of dejection as she swung her long legs into Mick's battered old car, taking care to keep her knees tightly pressed together, the way they showed you in the magazines. And her mood wasn't exactly lightened by the truculent scowl which was putting unaccustomed furrows on Mick's normally smooth, tanned forehead.

'You didn't tell me that *he* was home!' he muttered darkly as the ignition spluttered then fired on the third attempt and the car pulled away up the curving drive.

Daisy turned to him in surprise. 'Why on earth should I?'

'You know,' he mumbled awkwardly.

'No, I don't know. What possible difference should Matt being home make to me? He's not my guardian. He's just the son of my mother's employer.'

Mick shrugged. 'I suppose I'll have to get you home on time now, won't I?'

Daisy frowned. 'Why? Weren't you going to?'

His perfect white teeth gleamed like tombstones in the darkness. 'Thought we'd take the old Delaware road on the way home. They say there's a great view from there.' He leered suggestively. 'Maybe another time. How long's he staying?'

'Absolutely ages,' lied Daisy sharply, annoyed at herself for feeling so relieved that Matt's intervention had obviously tempered the ardent desires of Mick Farlow.

Or so she thought.

What she hadn't expected was for Mick to have the memory span of a gnat, and to forget about not drinking and getting her home on time. His eyes nearly popped out of his head when she took off her coat and he saw what she was wearing, and he immediately took her over to join a group of his friends she'd never met or even seen before. One or two of them looked distinctly shady and she didn't like the way they were eyeing her up and down, their eyes frequently drawn to her high bust and long legs. She fervently began to wish that she hadn't worn the dress after all. Oh, *why* the hell hadn't she listened to Matt?

She watched uneasily as Mick drank three pints of beer in quick succession, but immediately agreed to his suggestion of a dance. At least if he was dancing he wouldn't be drinking.

Which was pretty dumb of her. If she'd stopped to think about it, she would have expected him suddenly to develop the dexterity of a feeding octopus once he got her onto the dance floor.

As the dance progressed, Daisy grew more and more uneasy, and then she heard a ribald chuckle and loud whistles from his friends as he slid his hand down to rest proprietorially on her bottom. She felt quite ill.

'Get your hands *off*,' she hissed.

The fingers splayed out over one buttock. 'Come on, baby—you know you love it really.'

Repelled and beginning to feel frightened, Daisy tried to wriggle out of his arms, but he was a strong farm worker, his burly arms bearing testimony to the physical work he did all day, and his grip was too tight for her to release herself.

'Yeah, that's nice.' He leered. 'Do it some more. Move that beautiful body against me, baby.'

Really scared now, Daisy was nonetheless determined to keep her head, recognising with disgust that the struggle was exciting him, and that he was making damned sure that she knew about it. 'Will you let go of me?' she demanded with icy authority.

'Oh, come *on*...' His words sounded slurred. 'Sexy little thing like you—'

'Please?' she appealed.

'Just begging for it—'

'Or I'll scream—'

'Yeah, scream,' he mumbled into her hair. 'A little resistance makes it a lot more fun. And I'll sure have you screaming later. Screaming for more—'

Daisy brought her foot down hard on his, but since she didn't weigh a lot and her shoe was completely flat it made no impact whatsoever.

She bent her mouth close to his ear and spoke very slowly and deliberately. 'If you don't let go of me right now, then I shall use my knee to hit you in a part of your anatomy which I am assured is painful beyond belief—'

To her astonishment, he let her go at once, and Daisy searched around wildly before grabbing her coat and bag. Blindly, she ran out of the hall and into the cold night air of the December evening, every instinct in her body telling her to put as much distance between them as possible.

Her heart was pounding and her breath was coming in short, painful bursts which looked like smoke against the blackness of the night. At least the snow of earlier hadn't settled, she thought fleetingly as she stumbled along. She tried to reason with herself that she was probably overreacting, that Mick had just been a little drunk and over-amorous, and that he wouldn't actually have *tried* anything.

But there had been something so determinedly sinister about the way he had been holding her against her will that nothing she told herself gave her any comfort. For the first time in her life Daisy felt vulnerable and weak and abused. She had come up against a superior masculine strength which had been cruelly manipulative and had threatened her, and she didn't like it one little bit.

Haring down the road and scarcely able to keep her balance on the icy silver surface of the glittering hoar-frost, she almost fell into the public telephone box and scrabbled around in her bag for change. It seemed to take for ever to find a fifty-pence piece and with a shaky finger she dialled the number, momentarily disconcerted and then hopelessly relieved when she heard the curt, clipped tones of Matt.

'Yes?'

'Matt—' And Daisy burst into tears.

'Daisy?'

She made a gulping sound, waiting for his terse interrogation, but it didn't come. All he said, in an urgent and yet tightly controlled voice, was, 'Where are you?'

'In . . .' She gulped.

'Daisy—for God's sake just pull yourself together and tell me where you're phoning from.'

'The—call box.'

'Go into the pub—'

'But—'

'*Now*,' he ordered. 'And wait for me there.'

She heard the click as the line was disconnected, and she replaced the receiver as though it were a very heavy weight.

The pub, she thought, and looked just yards down the road to where the Red Lion was festooned with blazing fairy lights for Christmas. Dazedly, she could see the sense of Matt's logic—it was a far better idea to wait in the warmth and security of the pub than to stand alone in an isolated phone box—but the last thing in the world she felt like doing was having to face all the local revellers in the state she was in.

But in the event she didn't have to, because as soon as she pushed the door open the landlord's wife came bustling out from behind the bar and laid a plump, comforting arm around her shoulders.

'Come with me, dear,' she said firmly, and propelled Daisy behind the bar and through the connecting door which led to the landlord's private apartments.

Dazedly, Daisy allowed herself to be seated on an over-stuffed sofa, and obediently sipped at the disgustingly sweet cup of tea which was placed in her hands, while the landlady kept up a running commentary.

'Are you all right, dear?'

Daisy nodded numbly.

'Mr Hamilton just phoned. Said as you had a nasty shock, and that you were on your way over. Said that you was to wait in here until he came to pick you up.' The landlady sighed. 'Didn't talk for long. Seemed in a hurry. He's got such a way with him, Mr Hamilton, hasn't he?'

Yes, you could say that, thought Daisy.

'And wicked handsome.'

'Yes,' mumbled Daisy automatically.

'Always has been. Even when he was a little boy, I remember he had a way of looking at you with them big grey eyes and that bit of dark hair falling into them— Well, that look could have melted butter.' She took the empty teacup from Daisy's unprotesting fingers and put it on the sideboard. 'Terrible shame about his wife, wasn't it? Real beauty, wasn't she?'

'Yes,' agreed Daisy, again automatically.

'And him left with a young baby to bring up on his own. Imagine. Still, shouldn't imagine he'll be on his own for very long, not someone like Mr Hamilton. Oh!' She cocked her head to one side to listen. 'That sounds like him now.'

Dimly, Daisy heard the approaching throaty roar of a powerful engine which must definitely have been exceeding the speed limit, then the scorching sound of tyres braking dramatically outside. Then came the slamming of a door and hurried footsteps and there stood Matt in the doorway, big and powerful and commanding, a frown knitting his dark brows together and his grey eyes narrowed as his gaze swiftly swept over her, like a policeman assessing the scene of a crime.

And then he was with her, crouched down in front of her, holding her two cold hands in the warm comfort of his.

'Are you OK?' he said quietly, but she sensed the urgency behind his question and dumbly she nodded.

'Sure?'

Her teeth started to chatter, and he picked up her black coat and helped her into it, buttoning it all the way up for her, and then helped her to her feet. 'Come on,' he said, and his voice sounded almost gentle. 'I'll take you home.'

Home. It sounded like heaven. Like dreams she'd had for years. Home with Matt. Daisy registered that his arm was resting on her shoulder, supporting her, and the temptation to lean even closer against him was overwhelming. He was thanking the landlady now, and Daisy falteringly did the same, and then he led her out of the pub with such a forbidding look on his face that all the interested pairs of eyes which had been watching them dropped self-consciously to survey their pints of beer. Outside, he strapped her into the big, dark green Bentley and got in beside her.

He waited until the car had purred away before he barked out a question. 'What happened?' he demanded. 'The truth, Daisy.'

Daisy swallowed. 'Mick had too much to drink, too quickly. He was showing off in front of his friends. He asked me to dance, and he...he...'

'He *what*, Daisy?' His voice sounded very urgent. 'What exactly did he do?'

'Touched me up a bit on the dance floor.' It all sounded so tame in the telling. 'It was nothing—really.'

'Nothing?' he demanded incredulously. *'Nothing?'* His hands tightened on the steering wheel and he swore softly and extremely eloquently beneath his breath and Daisy was quite shocked; she'd never heard Matt *swear* before.

He didn't say another word to her all the way home, and when she risked a peep at his set profile it was hard, almost cruel, and unbelievably angry. She'd never seen him look so angry, either.

Daisy felt like a complete fool. He had warned her, and she had ignored him, gone and worn something thoroughly unsuitable to a small village dance. She had dressed provocatively, but the provocation had all been for one man, and one man alone, she realised. The man who was sitting beside her. 'Matt?' she whispered tentatively, but he shook his head emphatically.

'Not now, Daisy.'

She bit her lip, praying that the journey would soon be over so that she could crawl away to bed like a beaten dog.

As they crunched their way up the drive towards Hamilton Hall, she risked one more question. 'Where's Sophie?'

His voice softened by a fraction. 'Asleep. My mother promised to look in on her.' The car drew up to a smooth halt and he came round to help her out. 'Let's go in by the back entrance,' he said quietly. 'My mother will only spend the night worrying if she sees you've been crying.' He gave a bitter kind of smile. 'I've never known you to cry before. It isn't something you normally do, is it, Daisy?'

She shook her head. Even when she had been little she had had amazing resources of physical courage. That time she'd broken her leg . . .

She'd fallen awkwardly from a tree while Matt was home for the long vacation. She had been hiding from him, trying in her childish way to tempt him away from the voluptuous redhead he'd invited to stay for the weekend. It had been a long drop, and when she'd been X-rayed they'd discovered how badly broken the limb was, but Daisy had bitten her lip until it almost bled, she'd been so determined that Matt shouldn't see her cry.

She could still remember that funny smile he'd given her in the ambulance as he'd accompanied her on the drive to the country hospital, the way he'd looked at her as he'd said, 'Stubborn little thing, aren't you?'

Matt pushed open the back door and locked it behind them. 'Go and get into bed,' he told her. 'I'll tell my mother that we're home and look in on Sophie. Then I'll bring you something to drink.'

Daisy shook her head. 'I don't want to put you to any more trouble.'

He gave a small laugh. 'Daisy,' he said exasperatedly, 'don't you realise that you've been giving me trouble since the moment I first set eyes on you?'

After he'd left, it took Daisy ages to undress. She was still cold, unnaturally cold, and so she put on the thickest pair of oversized pyjamas she possessed, and was just climbing into bed when Matt walked into the room, carrying a tray, a reluctant smile on his lips as he caught a glimpse of her before she disappeared underneath the covers.

'Not such a *femme fatale* in the bedroom, then?' he mocked, but when he saw the look on her face the sardonic expression on his face altered completely.

'Hell!' he said softly, and he put the tray down and came over to the bed, sitting down next to her and taking both her hands in his, like a doctor reassuring his patient.

'I'm sorry, Daisy,' he said quietly. 'That was a pretty boorish and inconsiderate thing to say to you, in view of what happened tonight.'

'No, it wasn't!' She shook her hair violently, and it spilled in shiny golden-brown tendrils all over her shoulders. 'It's nothing but the truth, every word of it. I've only myself to blame for what happened tonight.'

'Blame?' His eyes had narrowed into watchfulness. 'What the hell are you talking about?'

'Just that you were right—I *was* dressed unsuitably. Provocatively. It *was* a stupid attempt to play the *femme fatale*. The dress was over-the-top for the occasion and Cheriton Village Hall *isn't* the place to wear things like that—'

'Oh, no.' Matt shook his dark head. 'Listen to me, Daisy, and listen very carefully. *I* was the one who overreacted about your dress. If it had been anyone else but you wearing it, then I would have simply admired it since you looked very lovely in it. But I happen to be rather overbearing and protective where you're concerned—I can't help it; it's something you inspire in me.' He smiled, and the smile made her heart lurch with longing.

'The dress was *fine*,' he continued. 'You were right. Women wear them all the time. Just because you look pretty and happen to be wearing a miniskirt, that does *not* give some lout with his brains below his belt carte blanche to start forcing himself on you, for Pete's sake. That's like those crazy judges in rape cases who have the nerve to say that a woman was "asking for it" if she was wearing something other than sackcloth and ashes.'

He stared intently into her mascara-smudged eyes, and suddenly let go of her hands, as though he'd only just realised he'd been holding them. 'So don't blame yourself, for heaven's sake. Do you understand?'

'I suppose so.'

'I want more than "I suppose so",' he said fiercely. 'I want you to promise me that you won't give it another thought.'

Daisy nodded. He was the most persistent man she'd ever met! 'I promise,' she said, and smiled back at him, unable to resist the soft grey blaze of his eyes, watching as he stood up and went to fetch her a drink from the tray he'd brought with him, becoming acutely aware of the fact that there was a man in her virginal little bedroom. And not just any man, either. Matt.

What had happened earlier should have been enough to put her off the male sex for some time, and yet it had done no such thing. She could feel a strange tingling of excitement prickle over her skin as she watched him move around her bedroom with that distinctively elegant grace. In the past, she'd simply acknowledged that Matt was exceptionally good-looking, but now her observation had acquired a distinctly new dimension. For the first time in her life, she found that she was intensely aware of all his physical attributes.

She gazed at the firm, hard buttocks and the powerful thrust of his thighs. He was all strength and power. Spare, lean flesh and honed perfection. Daisy shivered as she imagined touching his bare skin, knowing instinctively that it would be a combination of delicious contrasts: rock-hard muscle beneath the satin-smooth texture.

He brought over the cup and saucer and handed it to her. 'You're still shivering,' he observed, frowning, and Daisy hastily concentrated on her coffee so that he wouldn't find out just *why* she was shivering. The steaming liquid smelt unfamiliar and she wrinkled her nose up at him.

'There's brandy in it,' he said, by way of an explanation.

'I don't usually—'

'Drink?' he put in drily. 'I'm very pleased to hear it, sugar. But it'll help you to relax, and then to sleep. You still look really strung out.'

'Do I?' Daisy's gaze flew to the dressing-table mirror, and she was shocked at her dishevelled appearance. Even from that distance she could see that her face was as white as double cream, and that the mascara which had smudged around her eyes made them look like two sooty saucers.

She took a sip of coffee; it was bitter-sweet and pungent, but it made her feel marginally better and so she took another sip.

Matt sat watching her until she'd finished it, and then took the empty cup from her.

'Lie down,' he said, and he wrapped the duvet round her as carefully as if she'd been Sophie, and Daisy felt a sharp stirring of resentment. She didn't want him to treat her like a child. She wanted him to see her as she really *was*, as she'd become—a warm, living, breathing *woman*.

Her lips parted as she began to thank him and his gaze was drawn to them, his eyes darkening fractionally, a speculative look crossing his face, and he shook his head, as though he'd been mistaken about something.

'Close your eyes,' he said quietly, and she let her eyelashes flutter onto her cheeks. If this were a book, or a film, she thought, then Matt would kiss her. Tenderly at first, and probably on the forehead. And then he would give an impatient little growl because that would not be enough. His lips would find her neck, then travel upwards...inexorably...towards her mouth...

His voice came from a long way off; he was nothing but a tall, dark shadow, framed in the doorway. 'Goodnight, Daisy,' said Matt in an odd kind of voice as he snapped off the main light and slipped out of the room.

CHAPTER THREE

DAISY woke up to bright sunshine and a splitting headache, the smell of coffee drifting towards her and Matt opening the curtains, looking spectacularly casual and wearing the most faded pair of jeans she'd ever seen in her life. She closed her eyes tightly, not sure which was the most disturbing—the light, or the sight of Matt's superb denim-clad rear. He really *shouldn't* wear jeans that closely fitting, she thought longingly.

The curtains were yanked still further back, and Daisy groaned as the blinding light crept cruelly beneath her lashes. 'Ouch! Shut them, Matt, *please*.'

'No,' he answered unrepentantly.

Daisy slithered underneath the duvet, but it was ruthlessly pulled back and a pair of mocking grey eyes came into focus.

'I feel awful,' she complained, wishing that she were wearing something a bit more flattering than the ghastly pyjamas.

'You *look* awful,' he said brutally.

'Thanks, Matt.'

'Don't mention it.' He gave the faintest glimmer of a smile.

'With charm like that you should have been a diplomat,' she complained.

He smiled, properly this time. 'Drink your coffee,' he told her peremptorily, and pointed at the cup which was sitting on her bedside locker, then went and sat down on one of the window-ledges, staring out at the landscaped grounds.

Daisy sat up in bed and pushed the hair out of her eyes, then lifted the cup and took an appreciative sip. 'Tell me,' she asked him curiously, 'do you order *everyone* around like this?'

'Not everyone.' He turned then, his eyes glittering with mercuric brilliance. 'Only you, I'm afraid. I used to when you were young, and I guess it's become a habit. Why? Don't you like it?'

That was just the trouble. She *did*. 'Not really,' she lied outrageously.

'Tough,' he mocked softly, and closed his eyes to stretch as lazily, as a cat, and Daisy found herself watching him surreptitiously through her lashes, fascinated by the rippling interplay of muscles revealed by the simple movement. His stomach was completely flat, the leather belt buckled around the narrow hips. And yet the shafts of his thighs looked so long, so powerful.

Imagine them . . .

No. She was not going to imagine *anything* like that. Even without any particularly erotic meanderings of the mind, she felt her mouth drying and her heart racing like a runaway train. And oh, she'd been so wrong in wishing for some sexier kind of night attire. Now she said a silent prayer of thanks for the over-large, unflattering pyjamas she was wearing. They hid a lot.

And at least Matt was completely oblivious to what was becoming painfully obvious to *her*—that for the first time in her life she was feeling the slow, seductive flowering of sexual awareness. Her breasts seemed to have almost doubled in size, becoming heavy and swollen, their tips iron-hard against the thick material of the jacket. And there was an insistent tugging, an aching at the pit of her stomach, and beyond.

Colour flooded hotly into her cheeks, because she found that her thoughts had taken a wicked and totally unprecedented direction. She found that she couldn't stop imagining what it would be like to have Matt's strong fingers stroke and caress her there, where the aching was centred. To replace that frustrated ache with...with...

Completely distracted now, she drank far too big a mouthful of coffee, and scalded her mouth in the process, and discovered that she had been wrong about Matt being oblivious to what was happening to her. For when she looked up from her cup she saw that his eyes had narrowed and hardened, his gaze riveted to the heavy fullness of her breasts. He stood up abruptly, and suddenly she couldn't let him leave, not with that unbearable tension in the air.

So she gave him her sunniest smile, and saw the broad shoulders reluctantly relax. 'What are you planning to do today?' she asked, managing to sound neutral and efficient.

He hesitated, his brows creased in a frown. Funny, thought Daisy. She'd never seen Matt looking doubtful before.

He seemed to make his mind up. 'We're going out.'

'You and Sophie?'

He shook his head. 'No. You and I.'

'Me? You? Out?' Daisy's private fantasies were now threatening to get completely out of hand. 'Out where?'

He gave one of his lazy smiles, and a whole orchestra of violins started ecstatically tuning up inside her head. 'Have you forgotten what day tomorrow is, Daisy?' he teased.

'Of course I haven't forgotten what day tomorrow is! I've been practising carols for weeks. *And* my stocking is all ready to hang up!'

'So I want to go Christmas shopping,' he said. 'I haven't had a chance before, and I'd like you to come with me.'

'What about Sophie?'

'I'm leaving her here with my mother. I haven't bought her a present yet, and I want it to be a surprise.' He gave a rueful smile. 'Added to which I'm afraid she's totally impossible in toy departments!'

'Well, she *is* only a baby, Matt!'

'And I need you to advise me on what to buy for my mother; you know the kind of thing she'd like.' He gave her a steady stare. 'And, if you're *very* good, I may even buy you some lunch afterwards.'

Daisy's heart leapt like a salmon coursing upstream. 'And, if you're *very* lucky, I may just agree to eat it with you!'

'So can you be ready in half an hour?'

'Of course I can.' She paused, then sighed. Some things were difficult to say, but still needed to be said... 'Matt—'

'No, Daisy.' He shook his head. 'If it's about last night— '

'It is. I just wanted to say that—'

'You don't have to say anything,' he interrupted
gently. 'Let's forget all about it.' And then a grim
look came over his face. 'I don't imagine that your
friend Mick Farlow will act like that again in a
hurry.'

'He's no friend of mine.' Daisy shuddered. 'Not
any more.'

'I'm pleased to hear it,' said Matt, his mouth
still tight with anger, and some unaccustomed
dangerous gleam in his eyes made Daisy give a little
start.

'Matt?'

'What?'

'Matt—you didn't . . .' Her eyes widened as she
gulped. 'Didn't . . .'

He frowned. 'Didn't what?'

'*Hit* him, or anything,' she whispered hoarsely.

'Hit him?' Matt threw back his head and
laughed. 'Really, Daisy, you do have the most *vivid*
imagination. Of course I didn't hit him! If I'd hit
him, I'd have pulverised him,' he finished on a grim
note. 'No, I simply rang him first thing and gave
him the benefit of a few words of advice for the
future.'

Daisy shivered. Hearing that decidedly hostile
note in his voice, she wouldn't have been in Mick
Farlow's shoes this morning, not for the world.

He opened the door. 'I'll leave you to get dressed.
Hurry up.'

She was downstairs in twenty minutes flat and
wandered into the dining room to find Sophie in a
high-chair with what looked like strawberry yoghurt
lying in dollops all the way down her bib. Matt was
sitting in front of her, dunking carefully cut sol-

diers of toast in a boiled egg and handing them to her. Some of the soldiers *did* seem to be finding their way to Sophie's mouth, but most of them appeared to have fallen on the floor.

'Sophie, Sophie,' scolded Matt in mock reprimand. 'We really are going to have to do something about your table manners!' He looked up and saw Daisy. Was it her imagination or did he give a small nod of approval?

She had to admit that she had certainly thought very carefully about what to wear, in view of his acerbic comments last night. And even though he had later withdrawn them she'd decided that perhaps it was better to show him that she really *didn't* wander round trying to look like a *femme fatale* all day! In the end she'd opted for black jeans and a big sweater in burnt orange. She'd tied her hair back into a French plait with a matching orange ribbon and, with the minimum of make-up, the effect was scrubbed, young and innocent.

Only I wish I *wasn't* so young and so innocent, she thought suddenly as she helped herself to a slice of toast from the sideboard and smothered it in damson jam. If I were a bit older and a bit more worldly-wise, then Matt might look at me with seduction in his eyes, instead of the rather benign paternalism he always seems to display. She took a big bite of toast and wandered over to watch Sophie eat her breakfast.

The baby directed a pair of enormous eyes at her and cooed, and Daisy was instantly captivated.

'She's so sweet,' she sighed.

'She certainly is.' Matt glanced up at her. 'But be prepared to duck,' he told her drily. 'All the baby books say that you have to let them learn to feed themselves, that it encourages independence, manual dexterity, et cetera, et cetera, et cetera. What they *don't* do is warn you that a small child is capable of destroying a whole room by chucking bits of food round it! Sophie, darling, *please*!' he protested as a plump little hand jammed a piece of egg-covered toast into his mouth. 'It's supposed to be for *you*!'

'*Da*-Da!' Sophie beamed triumphantly, and Matt's eyes softened as he obediently ate it.

Daisy's heart lurched at the picture they made. Such a contradiction, really. Matt was the ultimate female fantasy: strong and dark and powerful. Tough, too. In business she knew he was reputed to be cold and ruthless—according to his mother. And he carried with him all the calm assurance of the greatly desired man. She knew that legions of women would adore to date him. And yet . . . sitting and playing with his baby, he was light-years away from the tough, commanding, sexy businessman. He demonstrated a gentleness that somehow added yet another dimension to his overpowering masculinity.

Sophie was a lucky child, thought Daisy with a sudden yearning, to have a father who loved her as much as Matt obviously did. She could scarcely remember her own father now. After he'd disappeared to India the occasional letter had come, charting his exploits with the latest guru he had discovered, but then the letters had dried up. And some years later they'd heard that he had died in a tiny mountain village—his health and body broken, but his ideals miraculously intact.

Matt had now put Sophie onto his lap and was busily removing all the little bits of food she'd daubed over herself, while she wriggled like an eel to try and escape the cloth.

'Keep *still*, Sophie,' he told her, in the resigned kind of voice which indicated that he wasn't expecting his daughter to take a blind bit of notice of him.

Daisy crouched down and began gathering up bits of toast from the carpet.

'Thanks,' said Matt. 'I was just going to do that.' He watched as Daisy took the cloth from him and began to scrub a small spot of egg yolk on the carpet, and when she looked up it was to see the oddest expression in his eyes.

'Is something wrong?' she asked him.

'Not at all,' he answered slowly. 'It's just that *most* women—or rather the women *I* know— wouldn't be seen dead crawling around the carpet scrubbing up congealing egg at this time in the morning. They'd be yelling for the servants.'

Daisy looked up, her fringe falling into her eyes. 'My mother isn't here to yell for, Matt,' she said reproachfully. 'If that's what you meant.'

'It isn't.' A spark of anger lit his eyes. 'Don't be so bloody dense, Daisy,' he said warningly. 'And don't you dare do either my mother or myself the disservice of implying that we've ever treated your mother like a servant, when you know you've both been like part of the family.'

She met his affronted gaze with a rueful look. 'I know we have. I don't know what made me say it.' But she did. It was the reference to the other women. 'I'm sorry, Matt.'

'Accepted.' But he was still glowering.

'Perhaps it's because I'm such a tomboy,' she said placatingly, 'that I don't mind crawling round the floor coping with congealing egg first thing in the morning.'

'A *tomboy*?' he queried. 'You?'

'Well, that's what you always used to say,' said Daisy, straightening up. 'When I was younger.'

His eyes were thoughtful as he stared into hers, which were a unique combination of gold and green, at the full, moist lips and the abundance of shiny hair which spilled down all the way past the lush curves of her breasts. He shook his head. 'That was a long time ago, Daisy,' he said quietly. 'Anyone less like a tomboy I've yet to meet.'

She had wanted a compliment from him, but now that it had come she found herself unable to cope with it, pinkening furiously, mentally kicking herself for her naïvety as she deposited all of Sophie's scraps onto the tray of the high-chair.

'Mother's in the morning room,' he said, standing up, and she knew he'd noticed her blushing. 'She's managed to resurrect my old wooden train set. She had me up in the attic at the crack of dawn, wanting me to bring the wretched thing down. She tells me that boys' toys are much more fun than girls' toys and that I must buy Sophie more! She actually accused me of being sexist when I told her that Sophie had no toy cars, only dolls. Sexist! *Me!*'

'And aren't you, Matt?' asked Daisy sweetly.

He threw her a warning look. 'Certainly not. And when you've finished cramming that toast into your mouth I'll be waiting for you in the front hall.'

'I was *not* cramming my toast!'

'And I am *not* sexist!'

Their eyes met for a long moment, then they both laughed with split-second timing.

In the brief but heady silence which followed, Daisy noticed that Sophie was watching the proceedings with interest, her grey eyes staring at Daisy curiously.

'Bye-bye, Sophie,' she said shyly, waving her fingers in front of her face, delighted when the baby gave a tentative little wave back.

'Ba-ba!' said Sophie, and Matt smiled his satisfaction.

Daisy's heart was beating like a frenzied drum. She was glad when Matt carried Sophie out of the dining room, and couldn't help thinking what a contained unit he and his daughter looked together.

Had the death of his wife hit him very hard? she wondered. He had been emphatic when he'd arrived that he had no desire to discuss it, but perhaps that was because the pain was still too raw for him to be able to bear to dredge up the memories.

It was true that apart from a newly acquired cynicism he still seemed very much like his normal self, but that was probably for the baby's sake as much as his own. You just couldn't let grief overwhelm you if you had a baby to bring up. You had to try and function as normally as possible. But who knew what kind of torment he experienced every night, all alone in the sanctuary of his room?

And Patti Page had been the most stunning woman imaginable. Not just a hard act to follow, an *impossible* act to follow, Daisy told herself firmly. Particularly for an eighteen-year-old with no qualifications and no clear idea of what she wanted out of life. And certainly not someone he was positively *brotherly* towards. So she should put any foolish romantic thoughts of Matt right out of her mind.

Which was easier said than done, she recognised gloomily.

Matt was waiting for her in the hall, wearing a brown leather flying jacket trimmed with sheepskin which emphasised the blackness of his hair and made him look like some movie hero playing a fighter pilot. 'You are refreshingly punctual,' he told her as he helped her into her coat.

More compliments. Much more of this and it could start going to her head! But this time, at least, she managed to keep the blush at bay. Good work, Daisy! 'Am I?'

'Mm.'

His hands briefly brushed against her shoulders as he held the coat open for her, and even that tiny gesture set off an involuntary little shimmering of excitement, her body flowering beneath his touch. She must be very careful today, she told herself. He really mustn't find out how she felt. There would be no Sophie there to distract them. And a man like Matt would not be flattered if he was aware of her feelings for him; he would be simply appalled.

Not only that. She must be ultra-discreet. He mustn't even get a whiff of the fact that she'd chucked in her maths course without taking a single exam. Now that really would set him off!

The day *began* well.

Daisy couldn't deny that it was fun to drive to

the nearby town in the most luxurious car she'd ever been in. Now she knew what Princess Diana must feel like! People kept peering into the windows and staring at them. Particularly women, she noted reluctantly as a stunning blonde did a double-take when she spotted Matt's darkly autocratic profile, then quickly thrust her bosom out.

They parked, and, after they'd bought his mother some delicate gold earrings, went to the toy shop.

'Let's get this bit over with,' he said, surveying the monumental pyramid of teddy bears which greeted them at the entrance with a wry smile. 'Sophie would have that lot over in seconds!'

A female assistant in a too tight overall spotted him and almost broke the land-speed record in the time it took her to reach his side and stare up at him with dark, melting brown eyes which made her look just like a puppy.

She completely ignored Daisy, the puppy eyes blazing at Matt like a car's headlamps. 'Good *morning*,' she said appreciatively. 'Would you care for any assistance ... sir?' she cooed, her eyelashes fluttering wildly, like a wasp trapped in a jam-jar.

Matt looked very mildly irritated by the girl's fawning attitude. 'No thanks,' he said, rather curtly. 'I have all the help I need.' And he smiled at Daisy.

Daisy gave the assistant a victorious 'hands off' look, and once the girl had wiggled away she and Matt got down to the serious business of toy-buying.

And Matt was a little like a boy let loose in a sweet shop, she thought as he began to pile toys into the trolley. 'Do you think she'd like this?' he asked, selecting an enormous doll which, it seemed, could not only walk, drink, wet her nappy and sing, but could also recite her tables!

'Perhaps this doll should be standing for Parliament!' quipped Daisy. 'It can certainly do as much as some politicians!'

'And what about this?' he said, pointing towards a very smart and very shiny doll's pram.

Daisy blanched as she caught a glimpse of the price tag. She picked up three brightly coloured plastic buckets. 'What about these? She can play with them in the bath, or in the sandpit. Look— one's got a spout in the side, one has lots of little holes in the bottom, and the third doesn't have anything. Very educational. And *terribly* cheap.'

'Daisy,' he said gently, 'I don't have to worry about how much it costs.'

'I know you don't,' she answered crossly. 'But you have to think about whether that's actually very good for Sophie.'

'*Good?*' he repeated ominously. 'Why shouldn't it be good for her?'

She ignored the warning light in his eyes. He'd asked for her help so he could jolly well have it! 'It isn't ideal for children to have too much. It spoils them and they don't appreciate it, and if they don't appreciate it they get bored.'

'And you're the expert on children now, are you?' he enquired cynically.

'Of course I'm not an expert—it's called common sense! You don't have to compensate, you know,' she added gently.

'Compensate?' he asked. 'Would you mind telling me what I'm supposed to be compensating for?'

'For Sophie's only having one parent,' she replied promptly. 'You probably tend to buy her more to make up for it. But you don't have to, you know. She loves you dearly—anyone can see that—and you strike me as being an incredibly good father.'

There was a long, stunned silence for a minute, and then he tipped his dark head back and laughed. 'Well, thanks for the glowing testimony,' he commented drily. And his eyes glittered as he said, 'You know, I'm beginning to realise how much I've missed you all these years, Daisy. I've never met anyone who answers me back quite as much as you do.'

'Your ego is big enough to take a bit of battering,' she told him sweetly. 'Now, what are we going to do about these toys?'

He gave her a heart-stopping smile. 'Well, as you seem to have taken charge of the toy-buying, you'd better decide.'

'The pram, definitely,' she said firmly. 'And a doll to go with it, but not that talking doll that needs ten tons of batteries to get it working. Buy her an old-fashioned doll which doesn't do anything, so that she can use her imagination. And the buckets. And get her that sweet little fire-engine— that'll prove to your mother that you aren't the sexist she claims! I'll put the rest back while you go and pay.'

There was an unmistakable glimmer of amusement in his eyes. 'Quite the organiser, aren't you, Daisy? You must tell me all about your plans for when you leave college over lunch. I shudder to think how our captains of industry will take to having you set free in their midst! I find myself quite pitying them!'

Daisy shuddered in horror as she went off to re-place his more extravagant purchases. Captains of industry, indeed! They wouldn't touch her with a barge-pole. What on earth would Matt say if he knew that housekeeping, waitressing or bar work were about the only things she was qualified to do?

Well, he won't know, she promised herself as she took herself off to the till, where Puppy Eyes was gazing at his platinum credit card as if she'd just found the key to paradise. The only way he'll know is if I tell him, and I'm certainly not going to tell him.

She shouldn't have drunk the wine. She most defi-nitely should *not* have drunk the wine. But two glasses of the delicious Chablis he'd selected and she felt as though she was flying.

She ordered garlic prawns followed by a pep-pered steak.

'Very adventurous,' he observed with sardonic amusement as he picked out his own courses—two exotic-sounding dishes involving huge amounts of coriander and rocket.

'I don't care,' she said, unabashed. 'I hardly *ever* get to eat out, so I'm going to have what I really like.'

'That,' he commented drily, 'is all about to change.'

She paused, mid-chew. 'Meaning?'

'Well, I wager that when you start university, or work, you'll be fighting prospective lunch-dates off in droves!'

That annoyed her. She didn't want him to be coolly talking of a future for her which included other men. She wanted him to be possessive and proprietorial!

'Why did you stop writing to me?' he asked her suddenly.

Daisy self-consciously took a sip of wine. 'I didn't think that it was appropriate—when you got married. I wasn't sure,' she added carefully, 'if Patti would approve.' In fact, she'd been almost certain that Patti would *not* approve. She didn't dare tell him that she'd been beside herself with jealousy that Matt, her beloved Matt, now belonged to another woman.

He didn't speak for a moment, and when he did he gave Daisy her first insight into what his marriage must have been like.

'Perhaps you were right not to,' he said slowly, swirling the stem of his wineglass between his long fingers. 'Patti was very possessive.' He looked up, his grey eyes very intense. 'Not jealous, you understand.'

Well, of course Patti hadn't been *jealous*—certainly not of Daisy. She didn't imagine that someone who had had all the glamour and fame of Patti would have needed to be jealous of *anyone*. Half of Daisy didn't want to hear any more, but she was woman enough to be curious about what his marriage had been like. 'What, then?' she prompted. 'If she wasn't jealous?'

He shrugged. 'Just that she needed to be the main attraction all the time. She liked to be in the spotlight for everything, even at home. I discovered that most performers are the same—they believe that they are the single most important person in the world. They have to, in order that everyone else should agree with them.'

Daisy didn't say anything; she didn't trust herself to. She didn't want to speak ill of a woman who was dead, but Patti sounded selfish, not giving. And not right for Matt at all. But that certainly wasn't an impartial opinion!

They were eating their pudding when Daisy managed to spoil the whole day, though afterwards she told herself that her indiscretion had mainly been prompted by Matt's unprecedented action.

When they'd taken the toys back to the car before lunch, she'd noticed that he'd taken a rectangular package out of the boot, which was wrapped in brown paper and which he carried with him to the up-market restaurant where they were instantly given the best table. She'd thought nothing of it.

But just as she was finishing her dish of mince pie with cream, and he was teasing her about having hollow legs, he suddenly reached beneath the table to retrieve the package and handed it to her.

Daisy put her spoon down and blinked, waiting until she'd swallowed the last of the pastry before she asked, 'What on earth is this?'

'It's for you.'

She stayed unmoving, staring at him in bewilderment.

He smiled. 'Daisy, one of the nicest things about receiving presents is actually opening them.'

She felt like a child who has just been told that Santa Claus doesn't exist. 'But it isn't Christmas until tomorrow,' she protested disappointedly. 'I'd rather keep it until then, if you don't mind.'

'It isn't your Christmas present, you goon,' he told her patiently. 'It's your birthday present.'

'But my birthday was—'

'Yes, I *know*,' he interrupted, a touch impatiently. 'Months ago. But I didn't get it to you then; I had a great deal of upheaval in my life at the time.'

'Oh, heavens, Matt—of course you did. I didn't—'

'Besides,' he interrupted again, 'I wanted to give it to you in person. To see your reaction.'

She gazed at him, her heart pounding.

'Go on,' he urged softly. 'Open it.'

With trembling fingers, Daisy removed all the brown paper to reveal what looked like a slim black briefcase. She flicked up the lid.

Inside was the most up-market computer she had ever seen. Daisy stared at it blankly.

'It's probably the most sophisticated lap-top on the market,' he told her, his eyes searching her face for her reaction. 'Once you've used it for a while, you won't know how you ever managed without one.'

Still Daisy sat there, staring at it. It was the most wonderful present she could ever have imagined, and she didn't deserve it.

Matt frowned. 'I know it's traditional for most girls to receive pearls on their eighteenth, but you're not most girls. You're the finest mathematician I've ever met, and this will be invaluable to you in the future.'

Reality crashed in as brutally as an ex-fiancé turning up unexpectedly at a wedding. She'd let everyone down. Her mother, Matt's mother, Matt.

But, most of all, herself. She gazed up into that angular, delectably autocratic face.

'Oh, Matt,' she whispered. 'Don't.'

The frown increased. 'Don't what?'

She shook her head distractedly. 'I can't accept it.'

Now he was losing patience with her. His look of perplexity was replaced by one of growing anger. 'Of course you can darned well accept it. If it's the cost—'

'It isn't the cost.'

'Well, *what*, then?'

'I just can't accept it, Matt,' she repeated helplessly.

'Would you mind telling me why?' he asked coldly.

'There's no point.'

He signalled for the bill. 'I'm not in the mood for riddles, Daisy. If you aren't going to tell me why not, then we'd better leave.'

Tears welled up in her eyes. For someone who supposedly never cried, she was getting a lot of practice lately! 'Because I don't deserve it,' she cried wildly. 'And there isn't any point in me taking it. I shan't be able to use it!'

He gave her a look of barely concealed ill temper. 'What the *hell* are you talking about?'

It all came out in a blurted rush. 'Because I've left school!'

There was a moment's incredulous silence. 'You've done *what*?' he queried, his eyes narrow with disbelief, and his face hardened when she nodded. 'How long ago?'

'Just over two months. I've no qualifications. I'm doing casual jobs where I can. Your mother's paying me to stand in for Mum while my sister has her baby. We weren't expecting you home for Christmas. You weren't supposed to find out.'

'No. I imagine that I wasn't.' There was a moment's tense silence while he digested this, and then he stood up, his face a tight mask of anger. 'Get up,' he commanded coldly. 'We're leaving.'

CHAPTER FOUR

DAISY had never seen Matt look so angry before. Never. His rage last night over Mick's drunken behaviour had been a mere drop in the ocean compared to the tight-lipped fury he was displaying now. Stony-faced, he marched her through the cold December streets towards the car park, one hand firmly gripping her by the elbow, the other holding the computer.

He didn't say a word to her until they were seated in the soft leather seats of the Bentley, whereupon he turned towards her, his eyes sparking icy fire.

'Right,' he commanded, his voice tight with rage. 'You'd better start explaining.'

The last spark of rebellion reared up. 'I don't have to explain *anything* to you, Matt Hamilton— you aren't my lord and master!'

'I want to know,' he said, deliberately ignoring her protest, 'why someone with your potential is now poised on the brink of obscurity.'

Daisy drew in an indignant breath, for surely his criticism of her implicitly condemned her mother too? 'There isn't anything wrong with housekeeping and cooking, you know,' she resisted stubbornly. 'My mother happens to have been doing it for years.'

'I know she has!' he exploded, his tightly controlled anger vanquished by a terrifying display of rage. 'But her circumstances were a lot different to yours! She married young and had you and Poppy. When your father left, with two children to support she *had* to take a live-in job; there was no alternative, not then.

'Your mother has had a happy enough life, but surely you aren't naïve enough to imagine for one minute that she wouldn't have been more fulfilled using her brain? You and I both know that she's an incredibly intelligent woman, as I once supposed you were. My God—what did she say when you came up with this little gem, Daisy? Didn't she try to stop you?'

'She did try,' Daisy admitted, adding defensively, 'Your mother tried to talk me out of it too. But I was adamant.'

'And why wasn't I told?' he said, in a voice so grim that Daisy actually shivered.

Because she hadn't dared to tell him. Because she had known that Matt of all people *would* be able to talk her out of it. And she hadn't let Mrs Hamilton tell him either. 'You know why,' she said quietly.

'Yes,' he agreed harshly. 'Because I would have damned well made you see sense.'

'You couldn't have *forced* me to stay on,' she protested.

'Oh, couldn't I?' He gave her a withering look, drumming his fingers on the leather-covered steering wheel as though he were beating a tribal drum. After a long pause, he gave her a cool look. 'So what actually prompted this suicidal action? What was it, hmm, Daisy? You needed money for dresses to go out to discos with the likes of Farlow, was that it? Did you sacrifice your brilliant career for the sake of easy money?'

'No, I did not!' she answered furiously. 'I don't know whether it's ever actually got through to you that cooking and housekeeping is not the best paid work in the world. No, of course it wouldn't have got through to you, Matt! I don't suppose real life ever does get through to you, does it? Stuck away in your ivory tower—'

'I live in a New York penthouse,' he put in coldly.

'Same difference.'

'Don't be smart!' he lashed out.

'But I'm not smart, am I?' she retorted. 'You've made that patently clear. If I were smart then I would never have set out on this, quote, ''suicidal action'', unquote. I wouldn't now be, quote, ''poised on the brink of obscurity'', unquote.'

His face remained set. 'I'm still waiting to hear some sort of explanation,' he answered remorselessly.

'You won't like it,' she warned.

'Let me be the judge of that.'

'All right, then, I will! I left because I—didn't—like—it,' she said slowly and deliberately.

'Didn't like what? School?'

Daisy shook her head. 'Not really, but *that* wasn't the main reason.'

'What, then? Your course?'

Daisy sighed. 'Oh, Matt—you don't understand, do you?'

'I'd like to try,' he said, his eyes as hard and gleaming as chips of ice. 'But you're not giving me the opportunity.'

So she tried to put it into words. 'All my life,' she began, 'I've been good at maths.'

He shook his head. 'No, not good, Daisy,' he contradicted her. 'Brilliant. Absolutely stunningly brilliant. There *is* a difference, you know.'

'Of *course* I know, and that's what made it worse.'

His dark brows knitted together; she'd rarely seen him look so perplexed. 'Made what worse?'

She sighed. 'The *pressure*, Matt. When you discover that you've got a gift for something—anything—it makes people very excited. It made *you* very excited, remember?'

'Of course I remember,' he said softly, and Daisy was reminded of all those times he'd set her problems, and been hugely amused and yet mildly irritated by her unfailing ability to get them right, occasionally even able to use her instinctive powers of logic to defeat *him*!

'It made my maths teacher incredibly excited,' she continued. 'Every time I walked away with another prize or the offer of a scholarship, he was almost more excited than I was! I used to think that perhaps he was living out his own frustrations through me.'

'But that's perfectly normal, Daisy,' said Matt, in a voice which had inexplicably gentled. 'Of *course* teachers get enthusiastic when they have an outstanding pupil. It is *tremendously* thrilling to discover raw, blinding talent. They want to nurture it, channel it.'

She drew a breath in, desperately wanting him to understand how she had felt, to know that she hadn't chucked it all in because of some foolish whim. 'I know. The excitement I could have lived with, Matt, and even the child prodigy aspect. But instead I grew to hate it. Maths, that is. Just because you're *good* at something, it doesn't necessarily mean that you have to like it; surely you can understand that?

'I could see this grim future stretching out in front of me. A life pursuing something I had grown to detest. Already he and the head were discussing my Oxford scholarship; it didn't even *occur* to them that I might not win it.'

'Of course it didn't.' Matt's fingers halted their drumming of the steering wheel. 'It would have been perfectly obvious to anyone that you would have walked it.'

'But I didn't *want* to walk it! The idea of spending another three years studying a subject I had grown to hate filled me with absolute horror. And I knew how much I was going to disappoint everyone. I became so miserable with the burden of expectations that I found I was actually struggling with my maths—me, who had never had a problem with it in my life. I used to lie awake at night fretting over it. And in the end the prospect of failing, of *really* letting everyone down, became too much to bear. Eventually it seemed easier to run away from it all.'

He ran his long fingers distractedly through his thick black hair, leaving it tantalisingly ruffled, and Daisy found herself itching to smooth it down for him.

'And how long were you feeling like this?' he quizzed her.

Daisy shrugged. 'A year. Maybe more.'

'Then why the hell didn't you talk to someone about it? Someone who would have understood how you were feeling?'

'There was no one to talk to.'

'There was *me*, for heaven's sake!'

Daisy shook her head. 'Oh, but there wasn't, Matt. Of course there wasn't. What should I have done? Telephoned you and asked for my air fare to New York and landed on your doorstep for the week? I can imagine how well that would have gone down with Patti.' She paused, and then met his eyes squarely as she said, very deliberately, 'She didn't like me.'

'No.' His eyes narrowed and he gave a nod of agreement. 'I know she didn't,' he added quietly, in a voice which, to Daisy's ears, sounded perplexed. She wondered if he would laugh aloud if she had the cheek to suggest that Patti had been jealous of Daisy's closeness to him.

'But anyway,' he continued, 'with something as important as that at stake, she would have recognised the need for you to speak to me.'

'No, she *wouldn't*,' argued Daisy hotly. 'Don't you know, Matt, that a married couple are a unit? That something happens when people get married? It's as though a sheet of glass comes down between them and the rest of the world. You can see them, but you can't get in. It's them against the world.'

He threw her a disconcerting look. 'You really think so? Then you have a very romanticised view of matrimony, Daisy,' he drawled cynically. 'And if that's the case, then I strongly advise you never to marry—you risk becoming sadly disillusioned.'

She stared at him, shocked at the sudden bitterness in his voice. 'Now who's being flippant?'

He ignored the question. 'All I'm telling you is that you should have come and spoken to me. I would have made it all right,' he said fiercely. 'You're like—'

'No!' she cut in quickly. 'Don't you dare tell me that I'm like a sister to you, Matt. I'm not your sister and I never have been,' she added quietly.

'I know that,' he said huskily. 'I was going to say that you were always my best friend.'

That simple declaration meant more to her than the world. 'Oh, Matt,' whispered Daisy on a broken little note that sounded too much like a plea, but she wouldn't go on—indeed couldn't go on. Because in a minute she would be telling him how much she loved him...

He looked at her trembling mouth and went completely still, the grey eyes burning with a message she couldn't understand.

She found herself studying him obsessively, unable to tear her eyes away, drinking in the sheer beauty of him—the gloriously high slash of his cheekbones which gave his face that peculiarly angular quality, the firm, sensual curves of his mouth, and the magnificent glittering of those mesmerising grey eyes.

Some unknown emotion prickled in the air as he regarded her with a similar intensity and it grew and grew. She was aware that his breathing was unsteady and that her own was ragged. Daisy wondered if he could read the desire in her face; but probably not, because the effort of keeping it hidden from him had made her features as tight and as rigid as a statue's. She wanted to look away for fear that she would give herself away, but found that she couldn't. It was impossible to break the magnetism of that stare.

He was so close to her that she could see a muscle tensely working in his cheek, and dimly she recognised that one hand was clenched into a fist on the steering wheel, the knuckles deathly white. There was a look in his eyes which she had never seen there before, as though he was fighting some inner battle with himself, and losing.

She felt the colour rush to her cheeks as, for one brief moment, she thought that he was about to lower his dark head and begin to kiss her. All the tension in her fled, her lips parting instinctively and her nipples immediately tightening with a wild, expectant excitement.

He surveyed her flushed cheeks, her sparkling eyes and the soft, parted lips, and he seemed to come to some decision.

With an almost imperceptible shake of the head, he turned away from her, and inserted the key in the ignition with a violent, stabbing movement.

'Put your seat belt on,' he snapped, and as she obeyed the car moved off with a sultry purr.

He drove with unaccustomed speed through the narrow country lanes, but Daisy couldn't help noticing that his knuckles remained tensed and white as they clutched the steering wheel, as though he were a drowning man holding onto a lifeline.

He didn't even bother to open the car door for her when they reached home; he just slammed his way out of the Bentley and strode up the few steps of gravel to the entrance of Hamilton Hall.

By the time Daisy pushed the front door closed behind her, she could hear the sound of raised voices coming from the drawing room. And she didn't need to hear the sound of her own name to know that she was being discussed. Dispiritedly, she hung her coat up. Feeling tired and headachy, she decided to go up to her room. Anything rather than face Matt again before he'd cooled down.

She heard the sound of footsteps, and Mrs Hamilton came out of the drawing room, raising her eyes expressively towards the heavens.

'You told him, I gather,' she murmured drily to Daisy as she approached.

'I couldn't stop myself,' said Daisy, giving a helpless little shrug. 'He bought me a computer— a...beautiful computer.'

'So I gather.' Mrs Hamilton sighed. 'I told you, my dear, that he'd find out eventually. And we both know Matt well enough to realise that he hates to be kept in the dark about things like this.'

'You mean he likes to be in the driving seat,' said Daisy caustically. 'Matt *has* to be in charge, doesn't he?'

'Well, there is that too,' agreed Mrs Hamilton, with the smallest of smiles playing around her mouth. 'I'm afraid that he inherited that tendency when his father died, but he was always strong-willed, even as a child.'

'And we all just sit back and let him ride roughshod over us!' declared Daisy. 'Why on earth do we all sound as though we're afraid of him?'

'Well, not *afraid*, exactly,' demurred Mrs Hamilton softly. 'I've always thought that he's rather like a headmaster. You know—you like them and you admire and respect them, but they're so formidable that they make you quake sometimes.'

'I'd rather not talk about headmasters!' said Daisy with feeling. 'I'm going upstairs to my room—'

'Oh, no, you're not!' came a silky contradiction, and Daisy turned round at the sound of Matt's deep voice calling warningly from the drawing room. Then he appeared, carrying Sophie and tickling her at the same time, but the eyes which met Daisy's over his daughter's head were as frosty as a winter morning. Little hairs prickled ominously at the back of Daisy's neck as she glared back at her tormentor.

'I'm going, I'm going!' said Mrs Hamilton as she looked from one set face to another, and she set off hastily up the curving staircase. 'I'm much too old for fireworks!'

Matt gave Daisy another icy stare. 'I have something I want to say to you,' he began.

'Don't tell me—you're sacking me?' she queried facetiously. 'But you can't bring yourself to do it on the night before Christmas—'

'Don't be so damned flippant!' he snapped.

'Why not? You can be!'

'I think I had a perfect right to be,' he ground out.

'So you're giving me the chop?'

'Of course I'm not!' he exploded.

'So what is it? Am I to scrub out the cellars as punishment?'

'*Daisy*,' he said warningly.

She met his gaze defiantly. 'What?'

He glared at her, and then there was the faintest upward quirk of his mouth which on anyone else

Daisy would have thought was the beginning of a smile.

But not Matt. Matt was *far* too imperious to allow humour to deflect his authority.

'You are absolutely *infuriating*, do you know that?' he demanded.

'Da-da!' exclaimed Sophie, and she started tugging persistently at his black hair. He stared down at his daughter silently until she had managed to coax a smile from him, and then he gave a frustrated-sounding sigh and looked at Daisy again.

'Oh, let's stop all this fighting, shall we?' he said impatiently.

Their eyes met for a long moment.

'You mean you've actually forgiven me for the terrible crime of pleasing myself?' asked Daisy sarcastically.

'Not at all,' he answered coolly. 'It's just that Sophie doesn't like it.'

And neither do I, thought Daisy suddenly. She seemed to have been arguing with Matt since he'd first set foot in the house, and she didn't like it one little bit.

'So. Enough?' he queried, and there was an irresistible light in the grey eyes.

'Enough,' agreed Daisy, wrinkling her nose up at the baby and pulling a face which made Sophie giggle. 'As long as you stop nagging me.'

His eyes glittered like sunlight on a winter sea. 'OK. No nagging.'

She stared at him suspiciously. 'You mean you agree? Just like that?'

He heard the disbelief in her voice and his own carried a dry note of amusement as he replied, 'Just like that,' he echoed softly. 'After all, what's done is done—all we need to sort out now is how best to remedy things for the future.'

'I don't understand,' said Daisy uneasily.

'Oh, don't you worry your little head about a thing,' said Matt dismissively, in the voice of someone talking to a complete airhead, and Daisy opened her mouth to draw an indignant breath but saw the mocking humour in his eyes and realised that if she was about to protest, then she risked falling into a trap of Matt's making. So she smiled instead.

The grey eyes glinted as they witnessed her mental tussle and semi-capitulation. 'Good. And now all that's settled,' he went on smoothly, 'I want to ask you a favour.'

And only *Matt* would have that kind of cheek! she thought.

She arched her brows at him. 'Oh?'

'I wondered whether you'd mind taking Sophie for a walk this afternoon,' he said unexpectedly. 'She needs some fresh air and I have some business calls I have to make. I don't want to ask my mother again—babies of Sophie's age can be terribly wearing.'

'Oh! Well, yes. I mean I—I'd love to,' she stumbled, ridiculously flattered and oddly shaken that he rated her highly enough to entrust her with the care of his beloved daughter. 'But will she go to me?' she asked anxiously. 'She doesn't really know me, does she?'

'Believe me, the very mention of the word "walk" will work wonders.' He tipped his dark head to one side and looked questioningly at

Sophie. 'Does Sophie want to go for a walk? Go with Daisy?' And he waggled his finger in Daisy's direction. 'To see the moo-cows?'

Sophie looked first at Matt, then at Daisy. 'Day-Zee!' she repeated solemnly.

Daisy exploded into laughter. 'What's all this "moo-cows" stuff? I thought that baby talk was a no-no these days? Politically incorrect and all that.'

'Rubbish!' said Matt with dismissive arrogance. 'Babies love it.'

'Then I'll take her with pleasure; the only trouble is that I don't know very much about babies. In fact, I know practically nothing.'

He shook his head. 'There isn't a lot to do, and you'll soon learn. She's had her lunch and been changed. Just try and make sure she keeps her mittens on; the wind's very cold. I'll get her ready.'

Daisy watched as with gentle hands he wrapped Sophie up in a bright red padded jumpsuit, corduroy bootees and a woollen hat with matching mittens. Then he buckled her into the buggy.

'Bye-bye, darling,' he said softly. 'What about a kiss for Daddy?'

Sophie puckered up her lips and planted a wet kiss on his mouth. Have one for me, Sophie, thought Daisy, and wondered whether the thought was written over her face because he gave her a wordless look while she struggled into her own slightly scruffy duffle-coat.

'The village tea-shop is open for the Christmas holidays,' said Daisy. 'I might take her in there for a drink and a bun, if that's OK with you?'

He nodded. 'That'd be nice. You'll need a beaker for her drink—wait there and I'll get you one.'

Daisy didn't hear him return; she was too busy playing 'peep-bo' with Sophie. The baby was giggling and gurgling uncontrollably, when Daisy caught sight of a movement from the corner of her eye. She straightened up from where she'd been crouching down next to the buggy to find Matt staring at her, the oddest expression on his face. For a moment there he looked almost—*wistful*.

No. Daisy dismissed the thought immediately. Wistful implied vulnerable, and Matt was many things—but never vulnerable.

'Thanks, Daisy,' he said slowly as he handed her Sophie's beaker.

He was being nice to her again. Oh, the relief to be excused his earlier criticism of her! Daisy decided to chance her luck. 'So it's all forgiven and forgotten, is it, Matt? My dropping out, I mean.' She tried him with her most appealing smile.

'Forgiven, certainly,' he said steadily. 'But not forgotten. We'll discuss it later, Daisy.' And he opened the front door for her.

He is *not* my keeper, thought Daisy crossly as she carefully worked the buggy down the steps and set off bumpily down the frosty path. And I am not afraid of *you*, Matt Hamilton!

Perhaps if you told yourself something often enough you just might end up believing it . . .

CHAPTER FIVE

DAISY enjoyed striding out with the buggy, listening to Sophie's cooing as she described the countryside to her, feeling a little shamefaced as she followed Matt's example and pointed out several 'gee-gees' and 'bow-wows', instead of horses and dogs. But, from her delighted chuckles, it was obvious that Sophie knew exactly what she meant!

In the village shop they had tea, or rather Sophie did. Daisy's cup lay cooling and neglected while she fielded pieces of flying currant bun. Afterwards she bought Sophie a book with brightly coloured pictures of farmyard animals and by the time they arrived back at Hamilton Hall they were both glowing and pink-faced.

Hearing the sound of voices coming from the drawing room, Daisy walked in, with Sophie cradled quite happily in her arms, holding onto her picture book tightly and waving it in the air like a flag.

Matt and his mother were just about to have tea and they both looked up at the sound of her footsteps, their conversation dying away instantly. And you wouldn't have needed to be a clairvoyant to know that they had been discussing her, thought Daisy wryly.

She stared questioningly into Matt's silver-grey eyes as he watched her cradling his baby, surprised by some powerful and unfamiliar emotion which crossed his rugged features; but it was gone as swiftly as it had appeared, and Mrs Hamilton gave her son a sharp look before rising elegantly to take the baby from Daisy.

'Come to Granny, Sophie,' she said, holding her arms out. 'And you come and sit down, Daisy,' said Mrs Hamilton briskly as Sophie began to wriggle in her arms. 'You must be worn out— you've been gone for ages. Matt and I have just been discussing tomorrow morning's drinks party, haven't we, darling?'

Matt's face looked forbidding. 'Yes,' he answered shortly.

'Naturally, the response rate to the invitations has increased by about a hundredfold since word got round that Matt's home,' observed Mrs Hamilton drily. 'The phone has been going all afternoon!'

Matt's face held a pained expression. '*Must* we have the wretched party?'

'I *always* have people in for drinks on Christmas morning,' replied Mrs Hamilton sweetly. 'They expect it.'

'Which doesn't answer my question at all,' he growled, then frowned meaningfully at his mother.

'Oh!' said Mrs Hamilton inexplicably. Then she said, 'Shall I take Sophie upstairs and change her for you, Matt?'

Daisy got the strangest feeling that it was a rehearsed question.

'That would be great—*if* you don't mind,' he answered, with a smile.

A hint of sadness touched Mrs Hamilton's fine grey eyes. 'Mind? Of course I don't *mind*, Matt. She's my granddaughter. I don't see nearly enough of her, and you'll be gone before we know it, won't you?' She turned abruptly and left the room, carrying Sophie.

'Gone?' asked Daisy without thinking, only aware of the sinking of her heart. He's only been back one day, and already I just can't imagine life without him. 'Why? Are you going?'

Matt rose to give her his chair, his eyes unusually guarded. 'Of course I'm going,' he said carefully. 'But only to London.'

'London!' said Daisy. 'When?'

'In a week or so.'

'So soon?'

His eyes narrowed. 'I only ever planned to be here for a short while over Christmas.' He paused as he poured her a cup of tea and handed it to her, but Daisy drank it without tasting it.

'What I'm wondering is,' he went on slowly, and his scrutiny of her was suddenly so disturbingly intense that his eyes resembled flinty chips of grey ice, 'what we're going to do about you, Daisy?'

She felt like an unopened present on Christmas morning that nobody wanted. 'I can look after myself,' she told him quietly. 'I don't need *you* to play nursemaid to me.'

'Well, I happen to think you do,' he snapped back, and Daisy started at the savagery in his voice. 'You certainly need *someone* to knock some sense into your head.'

'But why you?' she said, sweetly sarcastic. 'Because you're so wise and so clever? And so charming, of course.'

'Who else?' he responded softly. 'It's already been proven that your mother, my mother and your tutors all put together have been unable to influence you.'

She stared at him in disbelief. 'You can't *make* me do what you believe to be right, Matt!'

'Oh, I can, Daisy,' he said with quiet emphasis. 'And what is more I *will*.'

Daisy felt like hammering her fists against his broad chest in frustration at his unbelievable high-handedness, and she opened her mouth to object, but he silenced her with a shake of his dark head.

'Because if you continue the way you're going, then I'm afraid you're heading for mediocrity and disillusionment—'

'Don't be so damned pompous! Or so melodramatic!'

'And I'm not prepared to stand back and let that happen,' he continued as though she hadn't spoken.

There was something about his firm assurance which infuriated her, yes. But wasn't there something else too? Something so comfortingly protective about the way he seemed to be taking charge of her life? Hadn't that been what she'd always secretly longed for? Someone to protect her, to watch over her? And not just anyone.

Matt.

She found herself leaning back in the chair and giving him a stubborn look. 'So you're just going to wave a magic wand, are you?' she queried. 'Make me start loving maths again? Make me go back to school and move straight to the top of the class? And get heaped with honours that you and everyone else can bask in?'

'None of those.' He gave her a cool look. 'If I did happen to have a magic wand, I can assure you that I'd wish you right out of my life, Daisy Blair—'

'You and me both!' she lied furiously, her cheeks stinging at the coldness in his voice.

He threw her a resentful look. 'But that simply isn't an option, and neither, unfortunately, are the others. For a start, I certainly can't imagine you going back to school.'

Well, that was a relief! 'Why not?' she asked, curious to know what made him sound so forceful about *that*!

'Why not?' He gave a humourless laugh, and surveyed her with cynical eyes. 'Don't you know, Daisy? Really?' He sighed as she shook her head. 'You only have to look in the mirror for your answer. You're no longer a schoolgirl. Far from it,' he added. And the grey eyes swept over her.

She wondered how he saw her. As attractive? *Something* must be making that little pulse begin to work so frantically in his cheek. She knew that her hair was mussed from walking and that her cheeks were pink from the exertion, but Matt didn't seem to be looking at her face at all. Not once.

His eyes were travelling reluctantly down her body as though compelled to do so, lingering longest on the lush swell of her breasts, which contrasted with the slender curve of her hips and her long, long legs.

Daisy shivered with some dark, dangerous excitement. She didn't *mind* Matt looking at her like that, not a bit. In fact she positively *revelled* in it. Because it was not an insulting appraisal. There was nothing insolent in it, as there had been in the crude scrutiny of the boys at the dance last night.

She basked like a cat in the sun at the way he was looking at her. Because she wasn't foolish enough to delude herself that she couldn't now see a very definite spark of attraction in his appraisal. More than a spark, in fact. For a second there, she'd seen a positive *blaze* firing the depths of those amazing eyes which had now darkened to a stormy grey—the pupils as inky as a thundercloud.

He wants me, she thought, feeling briefly heady and almost drunk with her own sense of newly discovered power. He really wants me.

He'd wanted to kiss her in the car earlier today; instinct had told her that quite clearly. But now the eyes were unrecognisably hard, his mouth rigid with tension. He might not realise it yet, she realised, with a knowledge born of the same instinct, but Matt was beginning to want *more* than just to kiss her. He wanted to make love to her.

Daisy swallowed, momentarily out of her depth, both transfixed and terrified at the prospect of years of nebulous fantasies finally coming true. And another deeper, protective instinct warned her of something else: that to acknowledge the sexual attraction which she could tell from Matt's face he was fighting to resist would be to send him running as far away from her as possible...

Her voice, when she spoke, sounded amazingly and admirably cool. 'So school's out,' said Daisy, ticking off an imaginary option on her fingers. 'What else? I'm dying to hear just how you're proposing to save me from myself!' she declared.

Her nonchalant tone made him visibly relax. She saw the dark tenseness disappear from his eyes, saw him give a small shake of his head, as though he'd been the victim of some illusionary trick.

Matt sighed, glancing down at his hands, then looked up at her again, more earnestly this time, like a politician about to embark on a maiden speech. 'I accept that you've grown to dislike maths—'

'At last!' she murmured sardonically.

He threw her a black look. 'And obviously you can't be expected to pursue a career in a subject which you no longer care for.'

'But that's what I've been telling you all along!' Daisy objected, but he lifted his hand to silence her.

'The point is, Daisy, that you don't have to go to the other extreme. You're much too bright to do casual jobs all your life. Can you really imagine waitressing when you're thirty?'

What she wanted to be doing when she was thirty was living happily ever after with Matt, but there was a fat chance of *that* happening. 'Lots of perfectly nice people do,' she defended staunchly.

He shook his head. 'Few do it out of choice. You really ought to get on the career ladder, Daisy, or else do a subject you really *enjoy* at university. There must be something else you'd like to do?'

'English,' she said reluctantly, thinking that Matt seemed to be successfully talking her into something, and she wasn't exactly sure what it was. 'But we're in a catch-22 situation here, Matt—no university or company worth its salt would accept me without any qualifications—'

'*Exactly*,' he put in triumphantly, and Daisy got the distinct feeling that she'd fallen straight into a trap of his setting. 'So this is what I propose. We hire you a private tutor and you can take your exams in maths in the summer as originally planned. A little while longer doing the subject you hate won't kill you—not if it's just a means to an end. You've done most of the groundwork—it would be a pity to waste it all. And you've only missed a couple of months. Someone of your ability will easily be able to catch up.

'After that, you can do what you like—you can read whatever subject you want at university, or go into whichever branch of industry you want. And I promise you—' and here he gave a captivating, crooked smile which Daisy was mature enough to recognise as blatantly manipulative '—that afterwards you'll never have to pick up a slide-rule or a calculator again!'

There was a long pause while Daisy thought over what he'd said. The infuriating thing was that he spoke such sense, but, now that she thought it through, had Matt ever said anything which didn't make perfect sense?

She sighed. 'The tutor—that's if I agree to have one—will come here?'

His expression suddenly altered radically; his whole face closed up. 'No.'

Daisy blinked. 'No?' she echoed blankly. 'Oh, I see—I go to him or her, do I?'

'You won't *be* here,' he stated flatly.

Daisy was getting more confused by the second. 'I don't think I understand.'

'You'll be taught in London,' he said firmly.

'*London?*'

'Yes. You're coming back to London. With me.'

Daisy stared at him as though he had suddenly grown two heads.

'Say that again?' she asked faintly.

That arrogant assurance, which had momentarily deserted him, seemed to be coming back with all the force of a tidal wave. 'Certainly. You need someone to keep an eye on you, someone who can make sure that you're doing the amount of work you should. Someone who will keep that rather impetuous streak in your nature under control.'

'You mean someone like you?'

'Yes. Someone exactly like me.'

'To subdue me?'

He gave a glimmer of a smile. 'If necessary.'

Daisy was cross with herself for rather *liking* the idea of Matt subduing her, but the methods he had for doing so probably weren't what *she* had in mind! 'So you get to play nursemaid, do you?'

'Kind of.'

'And what's in it for you?'

'Ah! I was wondering when you'd get around to that.' He smiled. 'Plenty, as it happens. I need a temporary nanny. In fact, it will all work out rather well for everyone concerned. I have to be in London for the next few months—I'm looking to expand my business interests here. Having someone I know and trust looking after Sophie will enable me to take my time choosing a suitable replacement to take back to the States with me.'

Daisy's heart sank at the thought of him replacing her, and her mouth turned down at the corners.

He gave her face a searching look. 'I will of course pay you the going rate,' he added, and shook his head in mock despair. 'Since it seems that not only are you impetuous but that you also retain your notoriously stubborn streak. My mother tells me that you have adamantly refused to accept any kind of financial assistance from her.'

'Of course I wouldn't accept a handout from your mother!' she declared fiercely.

He gave her a cool look. 'The wage I will pay you means that you'll be able to enjoy the many cultural opportunities which London has to offer, while I will be there to stop you from getting carried away by any of those opportunities.' His eyes narrowed. She knew that he was thinking of her near escape from Mick Farlow last night.

'You're beginning to sound like a jailer,' she put in defensively.

'No, not at all. As long as you study satisfactorily, you shall have all the freedom you choose. You are, after all,' he added wryly, 'an adult. Or so you keep telling me.' There was an unmistakable note of amusement in his voice and Daisy knew a brief, but thankfully, resistible urge to go and plant herself down on his lap and start kissing him passionately. *Then* let him see how much of an adult she was!

Her cheeks growing very pink at the thought of kissing him, she gave him a steady look. 'Aren't you forgetting something? Something rather fundamental?'

'Such as?'

'I am *not* a nanny, Matt. I don't know the first *thing* about children. Especially babies.'

He shook his head. 'Ah, but that's where you are wrong,' he said, and his voice was so unexpectedly gentle that it tugged at Daisy's heartstrings. 'You know everything there is to know about children.' His voice softened even further. 'You know how to love them.'

Her heart gave a little tug. 'Matt—'

He shook his head. 'Just hear me out. Since— Patti—died, I've taken time out to be with Sophie. Just her and me, not even a nanny. I didn't even bring her here to England until now, and there was a reason for that. I felt we needed to get to know each other without any outside influence, however well intentioned. Just the two of us; I think she needed that and I know that I certainly did. And I'm sure that now—at least, I hope—she's totally secure.

'So it's time for me to start picking up the threads at work. Because I happen to own the company, I'm fortunate. I've managed to delegate satisfactorily. But now it's time to start gradually picking up the reins again.

'I intend to begin by working very few hours,' he continued, 'so that the change won't be too startling for Sophie. But those few hours will fit in with your studies, and with her.' He smiled. 'And she seems to have taken to you.'

'She's gorgeous,' put in Daisy immediately.

'And you like her,' he added. 'Which is the best credential you could have for looking after her. So. You'll actually be doing *me* a favour.' His eyes glittered. 'So what do you say, Daisy? Think it's a good idea, hmm? Mutually beneficial?'

'Am I allowed to refuse?'

'I'm hoping it won't come to that,' he said blandly. 'I'm hoping you'll see sense and accept my offer.'

Sense? she thought bitterly. Anyone with any sense would steer well clear of Matt, with his irresistible attraction. Anyone with any sense wouldn't harbour romantic thoughts for a man who had been married to one of the most sought after women in the world.

But he was right. Damn him; he was always right. What life did she have here, pursuing the kind of empty future which held all the lure of a plate of lumpy rice pudding?

Matt was offering her an opportunity to make her future golden; an opportunity to bring about change.

Anyone with any sense would manage to convince him that she could stay here and do it without him.

But she couldn't.

Or rather, if she was being perfectly honest with herself, she didn't want to, because she'd rather have a few months of Matt in her life than nothing at all.

His deep voice cut into her thoughts. 'So what do you say, Daisy?'

'Just one thing before I decide.'

'Mm?'

'Are you completely happy about the arrangement?'

'It was *my* idea,' he pointed out. 'Wasn't it?'

'That wasn't what I asked, Matt.'

Another guarded look masked the expression in his eyes. 'Let's just say that I have certain reservations.' He saw the question in her eyes and shook his head. 'But I don't foresee them causing any trouble, and I certainly don't intend discussing them with you now.'

But Daisy refused to be put off by Matt playing enigmatic. 'Why not?'

He sighed. 'God, but you're persistent, Daisy! Because whatever reservations I have are not important enough for me to let them jeopardise what strikes me as an ideal compromise for both our situations.'

Maybe he was afraid that she'd cramp his style, Daisy thought.

'And now—' he glanced rather impatiently at his watch '—do you want to learn how to look after a baby?'

Daisy nodded. 'Oh, yes, please.'

He smiled again; it really *was* like the sun coming out. 'Then come and help me feed and bath Sophie; see how it's done. But you still haven't given me your answer.'

Perhaps it was time to start lightening up. He *was* offering her a great opportunity, after all. 'Which part of London?'

'Hmm?' He looked at her quizzically.

'Would we be living in?'

He smiled. 'How would Knightsbridge suit you?'

Knightsbridge with Matt, Daisy thought, and felt a sudden uplifting of her spirits. 'I suppose that's really an offer no sensible person could refuse, isn't it?' she asked, and gave him a wide smile. 'So yes. The answer's yes, Matt.'

'I rather hoped it would be,' he said, with the cool assurance of a man who had never had an offer turned down in his life. 'Let's go and tell Sophie and Mother.' And as he stood aside to let her pass Daisy had the strongest urge to be just like one of those swooning Victorian heroines who fell helplessly into the man's arms. Would he kiss her *then*? she wondered, then sighed. It was all academic anyway. She was as strong as an ox, and had never fainted in her whole life!

CHAPTER SIX

DAISY awoke to a magical Christmas morning, because, after threatening to for days, the snow had finally been heavy enough to settle. She could tell from the moment she opened her eyes to an unexpected brightness, and when she flung the curtains open it was to see a picture-book scene outside. The countryside was clothed in a thick white mantle and there was an unnatural and beautiful silence which only added to the sense of unreality.

It was Christmas Day and, to top it all, Matt just happened to be home...

As she showered and dressed Daisy found it impossible to dampen down her excitement. She took care with her make-up and left her hair simple— gleaming and loose, swinging in a golden-brown curtain all the way down her back. Then she slid into an apricot-coloured dress which brought out the gold in her eyes. It was made of the finest wool, long-sleeved and high-necked and perfectly demure even though it clung to her slim body like a second skin. She stared at herself candidly in the mirror. *Definitely* sophisticated! But would Matt think so too?

You're mad, she thought as she pursed her lips up at her reflection then smacked them together to cover them properly in gloss. Stark, staring mad. But even pleading insanity couldn't stop the thundering of her heart at the thought of seeing him.

As she passed his room Daisy saw that the door was open, and she looked in. Matt was crouched on the floor of the adjoining dressing room, playing with Sophie, and he glanced up at the sound of her footfall, his eyes on a direct line with her thighs. Sophie kicked and giggled, but Matt seemed oddly distracted. 'Happy Christmas, Daisy,' he said eventually.

'Happy Christmas,' said Daisy, suddenly having difficulty controlling her breathing. 'Can I help you with the baby?'

'If you like.' He looked at her slim-fitting dress and gave her a funny kind of look. 'Although I'm not sure that you're really dressed for it.'

Unfortunately, he was absolutely right. Daisy crouched down with difficulty on the carpet beside him, trying to do it as decorously as possible, but aware all the time that the skirt was riding even further up her thighs. Matt's face became even more disapproving.

'I'll wear jeans next time!' she told him cheerfully.

'Good.' And it appeared to take some effort for him to turn his gaze back to Sophie. 'Ever changed a nappy?' he asked as he began to unbutton Sophie's playsuit and she immediately began to kick her legs and squeal with laughter.

Daisy shook her head as she leaned over and began to tickle the baby's bare stomach with her finger, and was immediately rewarded with a delighted gurgle. 'No, never. Terrible admission, isn't it?'

He shook his head. 'Not really—neither had I.'

Daisy laughed as Sophie grabbed her finger and tried to jam it in her mouth. 'Well, you must have been a fast learner, because she certainly isn't complaining.'

Sophie, chubby arms and legs going in all directions like a pair of helicopter blades, now seemed hell-bent on escaping.

'Goodness, but she wriggles like a little eel, doesn't she?' laughed Daisy again, watching as Matt somehow managed to get her to lie still for a minute.

A smile touched his mouth as a small foot bashed him in the stomach. 'It's because she loves the freedom. She's just started crawling and her idea of heaven is to roam around the place wearing nothing at all. Let's let her kick for a bit.' And he sat back on his heels and watched her.

He was wearing a suit, presumably for church and because it was Christmas morning. Daisy realised that she had never seen him in a suit before. Its formal lines suited him, the superb cut emphasising the sleek musculature of his limbs. And the severity of the snowy white shirt seemed to make his profile stand out in stark relief, emphasising the angular slashes of his superb bone-structure.

This is what he must look like every day when he goes to work, thought Daisy, suddenly getting a glimpse of a Matt she had never seen before—the successful industrialist, the rich tycoon. And in a way it made it all the more incongruous to see him sitting on his heels, amongst all the scattered baby paraphernalia. He looked thoroughly at ease with the situation, and yet it couldn't, Daisy realised, have been easy to adapt from busy tycoon to house father. Not easy at all.

'Was it very—difficult?' she ventured haltingly.

He threw her an amused glance. 'What? Learning to change nappies?'

Daisy flushed. 'No, I meant—'

'I know what you meant,' he said softly. 'I'm sorry, Daisy, I shouldn't tease you—but the habit of a lifetime isn't easy to break. As to whether it was difficult, yes, of course it was, very. At first.' He dipped his finger into Sophie's navel and tickled her, but his face had hardened. 'Oh, learning the actual *mechanics* of caring for a baby wasn't too bad—I mean, those are skills which are relatively easy to pick up. But doing it on a full-time basis I found ridiculously difficult.'

Daisy stared at his pensive profile. 'In what way?'

He was silent for a moment before he continued, lost in thought. 'I think that the hardest part was learning to slow down. My work had always dominated my life; it gave my life its structure. And that structure was about to undergo a radical transformation. Suddenly, I had to learn to live a life that revolved completely around someone else— someone who relied on me totally. And believe me it was some revelation.'

'And was the transition hard?' asked Daisy, fascinated by the insight, feeling closer to him than she'd ever been because of the confidences he was sharing. Oh, he used to talk to her at length, when he was at home on vacation from college, but this was entirely different. This time they were conversing as equals instead of as adult to child.

'Hard?' He looked at her then, and this close she noticed the tiny lines fanning the edges of his bright grey eyes which had never been there before, and the few silver hairs which nestled in the luxuriant black richness of the hair at his temple. 'Any kind of change is a type of rebirth, in a way,' he told her. 'And you can't have that without some sort of pain. So to answer your question, yes, the transition was hard.'

'But you must have learnt a lot about yourself in the process?' she probed.

Sophie gave a protesting squawk at having been ignored for all of five minutes, and a dry smile touched the corners of Matt's mouth. 'Perhaps. But I think that's our analysis session over for the time being, don't you?' he asked, firmly bringing the discussion to an end.

She felt suddenly and inexplicably shy. 'I'll put all these back!' she said quickly, scooping up an armful of plastic bottles and scrambling to her feet to put the baby lotion and the talcum powder on the shelf, self-consciously and yet gloriously aware that he watched the long, slender lines of her legs as she did so.

'Do you ever have trouble with your bad leg these days?' he asked suddenly.

Daisy shook her head. 'Never.'

'Not even when you're tired?'

'Nope. The limp has completely gone now.'

He smiled and nodded. 'I noticed.'

She watched while he cleaned Sophie with baby lotion then expertly snapped a nappy on her and put her into a clean baby-suit. 'There!' And he bent his dark head to kiss his daughter. 'Now let's go downstairs and see if Santa has filled your stocking, shall we, Sophie?'

Daisy smiled as the three of them trooped into the drawing room where Mrs Hamilton was waiting for them. Santa hadn't just filled their stockings; he'd obviously been working overtime, judging by the amount of presents which were stacked all around the fireplace, and the room was soon knee-high in wrapping paper.

After every visible package had been opened, Matt glanced ruefully in his daughter's direction. 'It seems you were right about one thing, Daisy,' he commented wryly. 'Sophie is enjoying playing with the discarded wrapping paper far more than with any of the presents I bought for her.'

Daisy shook her head. 'Rubbish! She'll love those even more—just wait until tomorrow,' she said as she shyly handed him the present she'd bought for him, which she'd been hiding round the back of the Christmas tree.

He seemed surprised as she held the brightly wrapped gift out towards him. 'What's this?'

Daisy found herself blushing—oh, but it was an infuriating trait she wished she could get rid of! 'What a question, Matt! What do you *think* it is?' she replied testily.

He shook his dark head in mock reprimand, the bright grey eyes glittering with unholy amusement. 'Now, now,' he scolded. 'It's the season of goodwill, remember?' He smiled as he pulled off the paper to reveal a hardback book, all glossy and new. Their eyes met. 'It's the perfect present, Daisy,' he said quietly. 'Thank you.'

'He *is* still your favourite author?'

'He most certainly is. I'm flattered that you remembered.'

If only he knew! She could remember everything about him, right down to his collar measurement, and if she'd ever known what his inside leg measurement had been, then she'd have remembered that too! 'You haven't already got it, have you?' asked Daisy anxiously.

'No, I haven't,' he said. 'And I usually wait for them to come out in paperback—so it's a real treat to read it in hardback.'

He really seemed to like it. Thank heavens for that. She'd been racking her brains, wondering what to buy him. Millionaires were not the easiest people to shop for—certainly not on her budget!

'I'll go and make some tea.' Mrs Hamilton smiled, and Daisy thought that she had the *oddest* kind of expression on her face. Almost smug.

After his mother had left the room, Matt reached into his suit jacket for a slim parcel which he handed to her.

'And this is for you,' he said. 'Since the computer obviously didn't win your favour.'

Daisy bit her lip. 'Oh, Matt,' she began.

'Shut *up*,' he said firmly, 'and open it.'

Inside was a pearl necklace. Creamy, translucent, exquisite—utterly, utterly beautiful. The breath caught in Daisy's throat and she stared up into his face, momentarily speechless, rogue tears pricking at the back of her eyes.

'Now, Daisy,' he warned her sternly. 'If you start crying over *this* present, then I promise you I shall never buy you anything, ever again. If you don't like it—'

'Of course I like it! I *love* it,' said Daisy falter-ingly. 'It's the most beautiful thing I've ever seen! It's just that I've never...never...'

'Here.' He silenced her stumbling thanks as he took it from her with a cool, firm hand to loop it round her long neck. Then he fastened the delicate golden catch at the back, lifting the heavy silken curtain of her hair in order to do so.

She looked up. In the mirror, she caught sight of the reflection they made, and the pearls which gleamed milkily against her pale skin were mo-mentarily forgotten because she was captivated by the intimacy of the pose they struck.

A man fastening a necklace around a woman's neck. Jewels which he had bought for her. There was something so intimate and so proprietorial about the way he held the silken strands of hair between his fingers that her mouth began to tremble.

Their eyes met. Some unspoken message passed from Daisy to Matt, was interpreted, and then, swiftly, he let her hair fall, pushing her away with a firm, admonishing hand.

'Hadn't you better see about breakfast?' he sug-gested, all the warmth gone from his voice, and Daisy realised in horror that he had said that quite deliberately.

Or had she forgotten that she was supposed to be taking her mother's place? And that included providing food for Matt and his mother.

'Of course,' she said stiffly, and walked out and along the corridor to the kitchen, where Mrs Hamilton was just adding hot water to the teapot. She raised her eyebrows in surprise when she saw

Daisy pull on an apron. 'Leave that,' she said.
'Come and have some tea first.'

'No, thank you,' answered Daisy. 'Matt's demanding breakfast.'

'Matt? Demanding breakfast? Are you sure?'

'As sure as eggs are eggs, if you'll excuse the pun,'
quipped Daisy as she cracked one into a bowl.

But when Mrs Hamilton had gone her hand kept
straying to her neck to touch the cool, smooth
curves of the pearls which lay against her skin.

The four of them sat down in the dining room
to eat breakfast together, Sophie in her high-chair
between Matt and his mother. Daisy tried very hard
indeed not to look as though she was ignoring Matt,
and yet she found it almost impossible to speak to
him in her normal sunny manner, aware that he
had deliberately created a distance between them.
She gave a heavy sigh as she pushed her uneaten
plate of ham and eggs away. Imagine what it was
going to be like living with him in London if the
atmosphere carried on like this, she thought
gloomily.

'Not hungry?' he asked in surprise as he observed her untouched plate.

'No, I'm not! And there's no need to make it
sound as though I'm usually a pig,' she answered
unreasonably.

'I'm not. But you hardly ate any supper last night
either.'

So he'd noticed that too. 'It must be all the excitement of Christmas,' she said lamely.

'Hmm.' He frowned as he folded up his napkin.

Daisy rang her mother after breakfast. Her sister's baby was still stubbornly showing no sign of

appearing, and after she'd made the call she and Matt, Sophie and Mrs Hamilton all drove in Matt's Bentley through the snow to the local church for the Christmas service.

The carols worked their usual emotional magic and Daisy didn't dare glance in Matt's direction, especially during 'Silent Night'. They travelled home mostly in silence, although it was punctuated every now and then by Sophie's squeals of delight every time she spotted a freshly built snowman in the gardens of the houses they passed on the way home to Hamilton Hall.

'I'll build you one later,' promised Matt as he slowed down to avoid a patch of ice on the road. 'The biggest and the best snowman you've ever seen!'

People were due for drinks at twelve, and Daisy headed directly for the kitchen when they arrived home. She had just started making canapés when there was a sound at the door and she glanced up, surprised to see Matt, his tall, lean body draped elegantly against the doorframe.

'Hello,' he said, the grey eyes faintly quizzical.

'Hello,' she answered coolly. 'Where's Sophie?'

'Having a nap.'

'Oh.'

He'd taken his jacket off, opened the top button of his shirt and loosened his tie, and Daisy's skin prickled in unwanted response as she caught sight of the small triangle of tanned flesh he'd revealed. Stop torturing yourself, she thought. And the way to do that is to stop staring at him. Viciously, she slapped far too much butter onto a bridge roll.

'Stop sulking, Daisy,' came an amused voice.

'I am not sulking.'

'Then why are you ignoring me?'

'Because,' she said pointedly as she gestured to all the bridge rolls which stood heaped in front of her, 'I'm busy.'

'Then I'll help you. What would you like me to do?' he asked patiently, and began rolling up the sleeves of his pristine white shirt to reveal still more bare flesh. Heavens. He had the strongest-looking pair of forearms she'd ever seen—sprinkled crisply with night-dark hairs—as strong and as rippling with honed, firm muscle as any labourer's. And even more tanned than his chest. Daisy swallowed.

'You can't possibly work wearing *that*!' she protested. 'It's a silk shirt, for goodness' sake!'

'So?'

'So you'll ruin it!'

'Rubbish,' he contradicted her calmly. 'I can work, and I will. Anyway, you're wearing your best dress—'

'It isn't my best dress—'

'Well, it should be. It suits you far better than that little bit of nonsense you had on the other night,' he added unhelpfully.

'I thought we'd agreed to forget the other night?' she demanded.

'So we had.' His eyes glimmered. 'But you still haven't told me what you want me to do.'

What she really wanted was Matt right out of the kitchen and as far away from her as possible, not standing there and tantalising her with glimpses of his body. 'I don't want any help, thank you,' she said stiffly, injecting the same degree of warmth into her voice as she would do if she were talking to a goldfish. 'I'm perfectly capable of managing on my own.'

He frowned. 'So why the prissy voice?'

She dropped the cheese-grater on the table with a loud clatter. 'It is *not* prissy.'

'It is.'

'Even if it is—so what? I don't need your help, thank you very much. I know my place,' she added, with a glare.

'Your place?' he queried.

'I happen to be *working*, Matt,' she said deliberately. 'You made it quite clear at breakfast where you expected me to be, didn't you? *In the kitchen.* So here I am. And I'd rather do it on my own.'

Ignoring her, he picked up a large prawn and skilfully began to shell it. 'I hadn't intended to sound dismissive earlier,' he said, matter-of-factly. 'I just thought it was a good idea to break things up.' His grey eyes were very clear, very direct. 'As they were getting a little...' He paused, and his eyes flashed out a series of conflicting messages. 'Complicated... wouldn't you say? And complications are something I can certainly do without.

'Now.' His voice became one of brisk efficiency. 'What shall I do with these prawns?'

'Don't tempt me!' retorted Daisy.

There was fraught silence for a moment. Matt seemed to be tussling silently with himself. 'But that's precisely one of the complications, isn't it?' he said at last, in a voice which was both reluctant and yet alight with some soft, sensual promise. 'That that's what you do do.'

'I do?' Daisy's heart thundered wildly. She'd thought so herself earlier, but to hear Matt actually confirm it ...

'You know you do,' he said acidly, momentarily very still as he took in her parted lips, the huge, darkened eyes and the little pulse which beat frantically at her temple. 'You may be innocent, Daisy, but you certainly aren't stupid,' he drawled. 'Only an idiot would deny that there's a certain—attraction between us.'

Her pulse slowed with disappointment. He had the knack of completely turning around what *should* have been a compliment so that it sounded like an insult. 'And you see that as some sort of problem?'

'Not really.' He gave her a cool, direct stare. 'Although it has the potential to become one. I'll just have to make sure it doesn't, won't I?' he added crushingly. 'For both our sakes.

'Now.' He gestured towards the table with an impatient movement. 'The prawns, Daisy?'

'The prawns?' she echoed in some confusion, still lost in the throes of discovering that, whilst Matt had grudgingly admitted to finding her attractive, he had dismissed it as something to be best avoided at all costs.

'What do you want me to do with the prawns?' he said, with the slow and deliberate patience of someone whose tolerance level was being severely tested.

Daisy gritted her teeth. She knew what *she'd* like to do with them! She'd like to tip them all over his dark, gorgeous and infuriating head!

Airily, she waved her hand in the direction of a plate full of carefully cut triangles of toast. 'Over there. Spread those with cream cheese, then put a prawn on each one, then a sprinkling of coriander on each one.'

'And where's the coriander?'

'In the fridge—I haven't had a chance to chop it yet.'

They worked in a tense kind of silence, broken only by Matt's drawled queries about the food and Daisy's stilted little responses, and she was relieved when he finally put his knife down. 'Well, that's me finished,' he said. 'I'd better go and sort the drinks out before Sophie wakes up.'

'Thanks for the help,' said Daisy grudgingly.

'Don't mention it.' The grey eyes glimmered. 'I can tell how much you enjoyed my company.'

Steadily slicing spring onions, Daisy watched him from between her lashes as he walked out of the kitchen, every graceful, elegant centimetre of him, and she had to put the knife down with a shuddering little sigh.

He had made finding her attractive sound like a troublesome cough he couldn't get rid of! He had said that it had the potential to become a problem. Oh, did it? Of all the most pompous things she'd ever heard...!

She was so determined to impress Matt with the brilliance of her cooking after his refusal to let her tackle Christmas lunch that she spent far too much time on the canapés, and barely had enough time to wash her hands, brush her hair and apply another coat of lip gloss before the doorbell clanged, heralding the arrival of the first guests.

And Mrs Hamilton certainly hadn't exaggerated
about the number of acceptances having swollen,
Daisy decided with unwilling amusement as she
watched the new arrivals glide hopefully through
the door. Word was obviously out on the grapevine
that Matt was back, since every eligible woman
under thirty was now tottering through the door on
heels which were much too high and impractical
for the icy conditions outside.

'We'd better have the fracture clinic on stand-
by,' whispered Daisy as she helped Mrs Hamilton
take coats.

'Don't be wicked!' answered Mrs Hamilton, but
her eyes were twinkling as she led the guests into
the drawing room where they all helped themselves
to glasses of champagne.

Daisy looked around the room. Matt was barely
visible; he was completely surrounded by a cluster
of chattering females, all tossing their manes of hair
back like demented horses, sticking their bosoms
out and laughing at anything he happened to say,
whether it happened to be funny or not. Daisy then
tortured herself by moving within earshot, so that
she could hear their tinkly little laughs and their
pathetic little observations.

'Oh, *Matt*—you really do say the most *dreadful*
things!'

'Matt, surely that isn't a grey hair I can see?'

'Matt, we're giving a dinner party *especially* in
your honour and I simply won't take no for an
answer!'

How he could listen to such sycophancy without
feeling violently sick she didn't know. Daisy

swallowed far too big a mouthful of champagne and nearly choked on it.

'I see he's as popular with the women as ever,' observed Mrs Hamilton drily, giving Daisy a pat on the back.

'It looks like feeding time at the zoo,' said Daisy without thinking. 'Or a pack of piranhas gorging on human flesh.'

Mrs Hamilton gave her a shrewd look and shook her head. 'You're barking up the wrong tree, Daisy. I wouldn't worry about *them* if I were you,' she said perceptively.

'I wasn't—'

But Mrs Hamilton had turned away to greet another guest.

Daisy stared down into her empty glass. Just what had Mrs Hamilton been implying? That she knew how Daisy felt about her son? And if she shouldn't be worrying about the fan club in the corner, then who *should* she be worrying about? Did she mean that Matt was still obsessed by memories of his dead wife?

An image swam into Daisy's mind of the last time she'd seen Patti—like a long, glittering blade of grass in that sequinned dress, the wide red mouth laughing and the black curls snaking down her back so that she'd resembled some pale and exotic gypsy.

Of course he was still obsessed with her. He'd loved her enough to marry her. They'd had a child together. She'd been taken from him suddenly and with brutal cruelty. And although some of the women who were now fawning over Matt were extremely beautiful they simply wouldn't hold a candle to Patti Page.

With a fixed smile, she went around the room handing out fresh glasses of champagne and offering trays full of canapés. Belinda Treherne, who was particularly glamorous and notoriously bitchy, looked through Daisy, pretending not to recognise her, even though they'd had riding lessons together for years. She was standing so close to Matt's side that she looked as if she'd been welded onto him, thought Daisy resentfully.

Belinda took a canapé from the tray which Daisy offered her and popped it between her glistening lips. 'Thanks,' she said, her eyes flicking disapprovingly over Daisy's clinging dress, before giving her a superior smile and turning to bat her eyelashes at Matt. 'Wonderful help you have, Matt. Quite difficult to keep good staff these days, isn't it? Absolutely *delicious* food, I must say.'

Daisy saw the unmistakable glitter of irritation in Matt's eyes as he listened to the blatant put-down, but she pre-empted any attempt on his part to defend her. She certainly didn't need Matt Hamilton to fight her battles for her! 'Then you must thank Matt,' she butted in, in a voice of pure syrup.

Belinda started, as though one of the ornaments had spoken. 'I *beg* your pardon?' she enquired haughtily.

'For the canapé you're eating,' supplied Daisy helpfully. 'Matt made them. He's *so* enthusiastic in the kitchen!' she sparkled, in a brilliant parody of Belinda's accent.

Matt threw her an amused yet distinctly warning look over the top of Belinda's head, but Daisy gave him a sweetly unrepentant smile and whirled away, leaving Belinda with her mouth gaping open like a fish.

Soon Daisy found herself cornered by the second son of a baronet, but at least it passed the time, which was ticking away with ominous slowness. He breathed garlic all over her and was clearly smitten by her golden eyes, or so he kept telling her. Daisy stood there listening patiently while he told her all about his misfortune in getting engaged to the wrong girl the previous year.

'Should've picked someone like you, Daisy,' he said, eyeing her up and down rather wistfully.

'But I'm only eighteen, Andrew!' she protested quickly. 'Far too young to ever think about marriage!' Unless your name happened to be Matt Hamilton, of course, she added silently.

And the black looks which Matt kept sending over in her direction and which were getting blacker by the second only increased her determination not to show her boredom, and to nod understandingly at Andrew at every pause in the conversation. Two could play at that game! Because Matt was certainly doing little to halt the seemingly endless flow of beauties who came to gather at his side, she noted acidly, even though Belinda was stubbornly standing her ground.

After all the guests had left, Daisy was just revamping her make-up before Matt took them out to lunch, when suddenly he came storming into her room.

She glanced up as the door flew open. It was a heavy, well-made door, but at that moment she feared for its hinges. 'Ever heard of knocking?' she queried caustically.

His expression was thunderous. 'Ever heard of playing the tease?' he countered in disgust.

She was on her feet in an instant. '*What* did you say?'

'You heard,' he returned grimly, and shut the door behind him with all the finality of a head-master about to heap punishment on the head of his most wayward pupil.

Daisy drew herself up to her full height and glowered at him. 'What the hell are you talking about?'

'I'm talking about how you seem to have the ability to project a combination of innocence and rampant sensuality; that's what I'm talking about. About turning those witchy golden-green eyes on a man and batting your lashes at him and parting your mouth so that it's just begging to be kissed, so that in the end he can't think straight!'

Hope dazzled in her heart. 'You mean—you?'

'No, I do not mean me!' he exploded furiously. 'I'm talking about that besotted young idiot down-stairs who has an IQ in single figures but who just *happens* to have a title! Is that what you're after, Daisy? A title?'

'Oh, don't be so ridiculous!' she told him scorn-fully. 'And anyway, I was *not* batting my eyelashes at him!'

'Yes, you were—damn you! I was in the room, remember? I watched you!'

'Then you obviously have defective eyesight—I should have it corrected if I were you!'

His mouth tightened, and a muscle began to move ominously in his cheek.

'Besides,' she countered, 'what about Belinda Treherne?'

'What *about* her?'

'She was looking at you as though she had a lot more on her mind than just *kissing*!'

'Don't be so disgusting!' he snapped.

'I just happened to be listening to what Andrew was saying. He was in the process of pouring his heart out to me—'

'I can imagine,' he cut in.

'Not—' and she stared at him defiantly '—that I think it's any business of yours, Matt Hamilton!'

'It *is* my business,' he ground out, 'if you're going to be living in my apartment, looking after *my* daughter—'

'You think I'm going to tempt her off the straight and narrow?'

'I want to know whether I am to expect the doorway to be littered with heartbroken swains!'

'Probably,' she said sweetly. 'But on current form I'd say that they'll very likely be female, and that if there's any heartbreaking to be done then you're the one most likely to do it!'

But her attempt at lightening the mood failed dismally. 'Don't be so damned facetious!'

'Then don't you be so damned pompous!'

'Good God, Daisy,' he said despairingly. 'Don't you realise the effect it has on men when you wear a colour which brings out the gold of your eyes, the delicious peachy softness of your skin? When your dress moulds itself so closely to your body that it's almost as though you're wearing nothing at all?' he finished huskily.

'Stop it, Matt!' protested Daisy, the blood beginning to throb through her veins in a slow, insistent pulsing at the hint of sexual promise in his voice.

'But that's just the trouble,' he whispered. 'I don't think I can.' His eyes were slitted, dark, dangerous. 'And maybe I need to do what I should have done a whole lot sooner, Daisy.'

Her heart was threatening to deafen her. 'What?' she managed to get out, her voice a broken little whisper.

He took both her hands in his, looked down at them for a moment, then up into her eyes. He didn't look a bit like Matt at that moment, she thought, quivering silently with anticipation. There was an expression in his eyes that she had never seen there, not in all the years of knowing him. An expression she had dreamed of over and over again, and never dared hope she'd see. Naked and predatory passion.

He answered the question in her eyes with a slow nod of his head. 'Yes, I'm going to kiss you,' he said huskily, and Daisy went very still. 'Do you want to know why?'

No, she didn't.

She wanted him to take her in his arms and kiss every last breath out of her. But Matt was tense and controlled, in spite of the muscle which flickered madly in his tanned cheek. And he was clearly waiting for an answer.

'Because you want to?' she queried, through lips which were drier than a tinder-box.

'Yes, partly because I want to,' he said grimly. 'But partly to exorcise this whole damned need.'

Her eyes widened in confusion. 'I don't understand.'

'Don't you?' He gave a humourless laugh. 'Well, then that makes two of us. I'm not usually at the mercy of my hormones like this—or at least I haven't been for more years than I care to remember.'

Daisy shuddered and turned her head away. 'What a ghastly way to put it.'

But, inexorably, he turned her back to face him. 'The truth, you mean? Plain and unvarnished? That's what you're objecting to?'

'If it's just h-hormones,' she stumbled, in a voice which was threatening to crack, 'then why don't you go and find Belinda? I'm sure she'd be only too pleased to oblige.'

He nodded, that same forbidding look making him look like the devil incarnate. 'Oh, yes,' he said softly. 'You're right about that. I could be in Belinda's bed tonight. Or even sooner, if I wished it.'

'Why, you conceited, arrogant—' Daisy tried to pull away, sickened by the implication, vividly imagining a naked Matt tangling Belinda among the sheets of his bed. And a murderous rage vied with a terrifyingly stark desire—to have him cover her body, take her, *her*, not Belinda. No one else, not ever again. Only her.

'But I don't wish it,' he continued. 'And neither do I wish to keep wanting you the way I do, Daisy.'

'Why not?'

'Because I can't think straight.'

Triumph flooded through her veins, but she said nothing.

He was watching her carefully, those clever grey eyes narrowed. 'And because it's impossible.'

'Why?'

He gave her an exasperated look. 'Hell... that damned persistence of yours,' he said, half to himself. 'Apart from the obvious obstacle of your age, and the fact that you will be living in *my* home and looking after *my* daughter—'

'I don't have to,' Daisy put in quickly.

He shook his head reluctantly. 'Believe me, if I could think of another solution to getting you through your exams, I would. But, discounting all that, there's something much more fundamental at stake.' And then, bizarrely, he seemed reluctant to say any more.

'Oh, please, don't stop now, Matt,' she said lightly. 'I'm a big girl now, you know.'

'So you keep telling me.' The grey eyes glittered. 'I wonder.'

'Just tell me why it's so wrong,' she urged.

He frowned, then sighed. *'Because I don't want to hurt you, Daisy,'* he said with soft emphasis. 'And what is more I have no intention of hurting you. Do you understand that?'

Which meant that it was one-sided. Daisy lifted her chin proudly, her eyes daring him to challenge her. 'Then, if that's the way you feel, you'd better go.'

'Oh, I will. But only after I've kissed you.'

She screwed her eyes up in confusion and he gave a soft laugh. 'But you just said—'

'Don't you know anything about human nature?' he interrupted in a murmur. 'Don't you know that if you put something out of reach, then it becomes unbearably tantalising? That forbidden fruit always tastes the sweetest? It's enchanted; it stops you wanting normal fare. And sometimes the only way to put it out of your mind forever is to taste it…just…the…once…' And he blotted the world out as he slowly bent his head to kiss her.

In a daze she took his lips to her own, as though they'd been born for that purpose and that purpose alone. At first there were tiny kisses, tantalisingly brief—kisses that had her arching towards him for more, opening her mouth so that his tongue could penetrate hers, so that she could taste him for herself, taste the sweetness of him.

He explored her mouth with breathtaking thoroughness until she felt that he must know it so well that he would soon stop. But he didn't stop. The kiss went on, growing more urgent and more intimate with every second that passed, until kissing was no longer enough and Daisy found her breasts jutting against his chest, their rocky tips insistent and impatient. He made a low moan at the back of his throat as he moved his lips from hers, his dark head travelling down, before taking one proud tip into his mouth and suckling it through the soft material of her dress.

Daisy's head fell back and she gasped aloud as blissful and overwhelming sensations fizzled like laser beams along her veins. Her hands crept beneath his jacket and with her nails she clawed softly and frantically at his back, wishing that she could rip the material away, feel the silk of his skin beneath her nails instead of the silk of his shirt.

'Tigress.' She heard him laugh, unsure of whether he'd actually said it, but she continued to ape those little clawing movements, sensing that he liked it. Hell, *she* liked it!

She made a small sound of protest when his mouth left her breast and she heard him recovering his breath as he moved up to softly kiss the long sweep of her neck. He clasped her narrow waist possessively, moulding her to the steely, masculine line of his body, and then, dropping his hands to cup her buttocks, he drew her very deliberately against his hot, hard arousal.

Daisy sucked in a wildly excited breath as she moved her hips against him in agonised need, letting him press her even closer, shivering uncontrollably as some heavy, pulsating sensation at the most intimate juncture of her body began to beat its primitive throb through her veins.

He reclaimed her lips and she welcomed him greedily, flicking her tongue provocatively into his mouth...meeting his tongue with her own, so that they fought some moist, erotic duel. 'Oh...' She felt herself shuddering helplessly as the rapturous entanglement continued, her hands interlocking frantically around his head, as if to pull him even closer to her. But there was no way to be closer, not with the barrier of their clothes between them...

He began to push her dress up then, rucking it impatiently up over her hips, so that the flat of his hand was on her bare flesh, rapidly moving and learning its contours through touch alone as it circled the planes of her flat stomach. And she knew what she wanted him to do even before he started skimming his fingers down to hook them inside the lacy panels at the sides of her panties, before starting to slide them over her narrow hips.

She arched invitingly, pleadingly, and he traced tiny, light circles with his fingertips at the tops of her thighs, tormenting her until she could bear it no longer. 'Please,' she begged him, scarcely aware of what she was saying. 'Please, Matt—'

He lifted her off her feet, carried her the short distance to the bed and pushed her down onto it, his face dark and tight and almost cruel with passion.

'I want you, Daisy,' he said unsteadily. 'God forgive me, but I want you. What enchantment have you cast over me, sweetheart? I'm powerless in your arms, don't you know that? You're so beautiful, so very, very beautiful, and I can't resist you. So stop me, sweetheart ... send me away...'

'No,' she whispered back, unable to prevent the smile of delight from stealing over the softness of her mouth as she registered the term of endearment he'd used. 'I don't want you to stop,' she heard herself saying, her voice sounding strangely indistinct because her mouth was swollen from all that kissing. 'I want you to make love to me, Matt. More than anything else in the world.'

Unwittingly her hand brushed against the swollen hardness of his arousal and she heard him utter some terse profanity that sounded like intense enjoyment. So she touched him there again and this time she felt him shudder with helpless pleasure.

'Dear heaven, don't,' he whispered.

'Why? Don't you like it?'

'You know I do,' he answered, and he ran his hands possessively over her hips. 'You know I do.'

Matt's hands were now sliding deliciously all over the tops of her legs and she was starting to pull frantically at his belt when a loud cry stilled them both into intertwined statues.

Sophie.

For a second, it was like being suspended in time. They lay frozen in motion, Matt's hands still splayed proprietorially over her inner thighs, Daisy's fingers clutching at the buckle of the belt.

His hands suddenly left her as though they had been touching poison and he closed his eyes briefly. When he opened them again, he seemed to have aged by about five years. Daisy found herself recoiling from the expression of icy distaste which was etched hard and unforgivingly onto his features. He looked, she thought, like a man who had just had a glimpse of hell and been promised an eternity there.

And there was recrimination, too, blazing like bright fire from his smoky grey eyes as he roughly levered her up by her shoulders. 'For Pete's sake, Daisy!' he exploded fiercely. 'How many men have you done that with? How many men have you let undress you and touch you there? Kiss your breasts as I just did?'

'Matt!' she gasped in disbelief, but he shook his dark head wildly and carried on, like a man possessed.

'If Sophie hadn't stopped us,' he stormed, 'I would have been making love to you right now, wouldn't I? How many men, Daisy? For God's sake—*tell me!*'

Daisy drew in a shuddering breath, sickened to the stomach by his accusation, her hands ineffectually pushing him away. 'How dare you?' she retaliated shakily. 'You have no right to ask me something like that after what you've just done. No right to speak to me as though I were little more than some kind of—*tramp*.' She spat the last word out and he winced.

He expelled a long, tense sigh, and then he let her go, allowing her to fall back against the softness of the pillows as he moved away from her bed. He stood silently for a moment and looked down at her, his face an uncomfortable mixture of regret and self-contempt. And frustration.

'You're right,' he said finally, in a cool, flat tone, and that in a way was far worse than what he had said before, because Daisy would rather have had the passion, and the anger, than this indifferent coldness.

He spoke the words like a judge pronouncing sentence. 'My behaviour towards you has been inexcusable, Daisy,' he said very softly. 'Firstly in almost ravishing you like that, and secondly in the brutal and totally unfair accusation about your morals, which I had no right to make.'

'No, you didn't!' agreed Daisy furiously, and she pushed back her mussed hair agitatedly.

'Because what you've done,' he continued, 'and with whom, is absolutely none of my business.'

That made her sit up, lifting her chin defiantly. 'Oh, don't talk such rubbish, Matt,' she told him scornfully. 'You know damned well there hasn't been any other man!'

Their eyes met and there was a tense, brittle silence as he acknowledged her virginity. He expelled a long breath, some indeterminate glitter firing the depths of his grey eyes. 'Yes, I know that,' he said eventually. 'But a man can say some pretty foolish things when he's in this kind of—' He grimaced, and he didn't have to complete the sentence for Daisy to know what he meant because she was just as frustrated as he was.

He shook his head. 'It doesn't matter—not now, anyway. The whole incident is best forgotten.'

'*Forgotten?*' Daisy echoed incredulously. How on earth could he *forget* what had happened?

His eyes narrowed decisively. 'Yes, forgotten,' he told her forbiddingly.

Daisy didn't know whether his women normally fought for what they wanted, but she didn't care. *She* was about to!

'But I wanted you to "ravish" me!' she protested, her cheeks burning with embarrassment. 'I wanted you to make love to me just as much as you wanted it, Matt! Is that so very wrong?'

He shook his head impatiently. 'Not exactly wrong. Inappropriate would be a better word.' His mouth curved into a hard semicircle of contempt. 'My God,' he whispered incredulously, half to himself. 'I can't believe what I almost did. I behaved like some kind of . . . some kind of . . .'

'Oh, for goodness' sake will you stop blaming yourself?' beseeched Daisy, going cold at the look on his face as he gave her an icily questioning stare. 'And don't stare at me like that! It's no sin, no crime. It's—'

'It's never going to happen again, Daisy,' he said grimly. 'Do you understand that?'

Her mouth trembling, she stared back at him defiantly.

'Do you?' he repeated ominously.

Still she said nothing; she couldn't trust herself not to do or say something totally ridiculous.

'I don't feel proud of what has just taken place,' he said, the sombre voice of the judge back again, only this time the sentence he was pronouncing sounded very like a death sentence. 'But you can rest assured that there will be no repeat of it.'

But she didn't want to rest assured! She *wanted* a repeat of it! She wanted him to finish making love to her—maybe not now, but certainly some time in the future! She was in love with the man and had been for as long as she could remember, for goodness' sake! 'But Matt—'

But he shook his head in negation, and without a word he leaned over the bed and pulled her panties back up with a slick, experienced movement which filled her with jealousy.

'Now get up, Daisy,' he ordered quietly. 'We have a table booked for lunch. I have Sophie to see to, and my mother will be downstairs wondering what's happened to us.'

Guilty colour flooded Daisy's cheeks as she stared up at him in silent horror. Dear Lord! Her room had been unlocked! Mrs Hamilton could have walked in on them at any time!

'Yes,' he said wearily, but the forbidding look in his eyes devastated her. 'And I hope to God she doesn't begin to guess. Now get up,' he urged again, more urgently this time, and with shaky legs Daisy complied.

His eyes swept over her in cold assessment, lingering on the two damp circles at her breasts where he'd suckled her, and his mouth thinned with contempt. 'You'd better change your dress,' he said curtly. 'You can't go out for lunch looking like that.'

After the door had closed behind him, Daisy sank down again on the bed, her knees too weak to hold her, feeling aching and frustrated, and as angry as hell.

CHAPTER SEVEN

DAISY sat in the sitting room of Matt's London apartment and waited for him to finish putting Sophie to bed.

It was the most gorgeous place she'd ever seen, she thought wistfully as she let her gaze wander round. And what a view! It was one of those rare, very old-fashioned flats, with high, airy rooms and dramatically beautiful proportions and virtually every original feature left intact.

She'd wondered aloud in the car on the journey down why Matt bothered having an apartment in London if he lived in New York.

'It's an investment—I own properties all over the world,' he'd replied shortly. 'I've only recently bought it.'

'What—already decorated?' Daisy had asked curiously.

He'd shaken his head. 'I had my assistant fly over to decorate and furnish it for me—she knows my taste pretty well.'

She? Daisy had stiffened. 'Oh,' she'd said slowly. 'That must be nice for you—to have someone know your taste so well.'

'Yes,' he'd agreed succinctly. 'Barbara's the epitome of efficiency.' And then, repressively, he'd asked, 'Daisy, do you *mind*? I'm trying to concentrate on the road.'

Daisy glanced up and smiled as Matt walked into the sitting room, but her smile met with the now familiar stony response.

She sighed. Surely a little peace-making wouldn't go amiss? Because one week after that disastrous episode with Matt in her bedroom relations with him remained at an all-time and extremely frosty low. She perched on the edge of the dark blue silk sofa and cleared her throat. 'It's an—er—absolutely gorgeous apartment, Matt. Wonderful. I love that sculpture over in the corner.' And Barbara, his assistant, obviously knew his taste *very* well, if she'd been the purchaser of something as intimate as *that*! she thought.

'Thanks. It's adequate. And on the plus side it's large enough—' his eyes flashed some warning message '—for us to live here together without falling over each other every minute.'

'You mean that you intend to continue virtually ignoring me as you have done since—?'

'Since the day I nearly made love to you?' he put in brutally. 'Yes. Does it give you some kind of kick to keep reminding me of it, Daisy?'

'Oh, don't be so *ridiculous*!' Daisy slammed her fist against her thigh, which had been respectably covered in either leggings or jeans ever since he'd gone on about the seductive qualities of close-fitting apricot-coloured dresses, because she certainly wasn't going to be accused of attempting to seduce him. Much as she might be tempted, she had no intention of laying herself open to his scornful refusal. Not again. 'No, it does not give me some sort of kick! How warped can you get? I just think that it's crazy to carry on the way we have been—'

'I just want to *forget* it ever happened—can't you get that into your head?' he interrupted savagely.

'But we can't forget it ever happened if you're going to keep avoiding me like the plague, can we?' protested Daisy. 'Every time I walk into a room, you walk out. I was beginning to wonder whether I ought to change my deodorant.'

'That's an exaggeration,' he put in tersely, but Daisy could see that he was trying very hard not to laugh.

Sensing partial capitulation, she battled on. 'Well, maybe a *bit* of an exaggeration, but you know what I mean, Matt. Can't we just go back to being like we used to be?'

'I don't know,' he said slowly and honestly. 'I'm not so sure that we can.'

Daisy felt as though someone had whipped the carpet out from under her feet. 'You mean all those years of friendship now mean nothing? Destroyed by—?

'Lust?' he queried callously.

'Matt—'

'And don't say Matt like that!' he told her exasperatedly, and this sudden glimpse of the old Matt he'd been hiding beneath the mask of a stranger all week gave Daisy renewed confidence.

'Like what?' she enquired hopefully.

'Like you used to when you were a little girl.'

'And how was that?' she put in quickly, clinging like a limpet to any hint of a truce.

'All wide-eyed. As though I was some strong, powerful, omnipotent being who could do no wrong; who could make everything right in the world for you.'

'Oh, my.' She met his smouldering eyes with a mocking gaze of her own. 'I may still be relatively young, Matt, but I'm no longer quite so naïve as to believe *that*.'

There was a glimmer of answering humour in his smile. 'And that remark, I suppose, was intended to put me very firmly in my place.'

'Perhaps you need to be put very firmly in your place,' she said softly.

'Perhaps I do.' He stared at her for a moment, then walked over to a cabinet at one side of the room where he poured himself a whisky and soda, and took a long and thoughtful mouthful.

'Aren't you going to offer *me* a drink?'

'I'm sorry. Would you like some tea, or coffee, perhaps?'

'How about a beaker full of warm milk?' she queried acidly. 'I'm not Sophie, Matt—I'll have whatever it is that you're having.'

'I'd rather you didn't,' he said stubbornly. 'I don't want you getting hooked on hard liquor—'

'As well as on sex?'

'That does it! Is *nothing* sacred to you?' He slammed his glass down on the cabinet so violently that Daisy was amazed it didn't shatter. 'You know,' he said, with feeling, 'you really are the most infuriating person I have ever met!'

'Snap! Only to my assessment of you I'd add unbearably arrogant and conceited—'

'Must you always answer back?' he demanded exasperatedly. 'You always seem to have some smart answer for everything. Or think you have!'

'Snap!' she said again.

He sighed heavily as he met her belligerent gaze. 'You know, this isn't going to work.'

'What isn't?'

'Having you here.' He raised his whisky to his mouth, looked at her raised eyebrows, and put it down untouched. 'Wait here,' he instructed with a glower.

Minutes later, he reappeared, carrying a loaded tea-tray. He poured them both a cup of tea and handed one gravely to Daisy. 'And you can wipe that self-satisfied expression off your face,' he told her severely.

'Yes, Matt,' she answered demurely, and sipped at the tea.

He drank his own in silence for a while. 'Perhaps it might be better,' he said eventually, 'if I arranged for you to have the tuition, but to live somewhere else.'

'But I thought you didn't trust me to work except under your own censorious eye,' observed Daisy sarcastically.

'Perhaps with hindsight I've decided that my trust might have been rather misplaced. I think that in view of this rather inconvenient...' He hesitated.

'Mm?' she pursued ruthlessly.

'Attraction...' he ground out, as though he'd been forced to swallow snake poison. So it hadn't gone away entirely, thought Daisy delightedly. 'That it might be preferable for you to live somewhere else.'

'But there's Sophie to consider,' Daisy objected. 'Part of the deal was that I was to look after her.'

He shook his head. 'I can find someone else to look after Sophie. Don't worry about that.'

'And I don't have any income,' she pointed out, but he shook his head again impatiently.

'That's of no consequence,' he said dismissively, and Daisy suddenly bristled with indignation at his high-handedness. He was trying to move people around like chess pieces, for heaven's sake!

She put her cup down on the table. 'Well, maybe it isn't of consequence to you, but I'm not having you set me up in a flat—like a mistress, only without any of the obvious perks! I'd rather earn my keep by helping care for Sophie. Besides which, I like her.' She paused, and when she spoke it was with great emphasis. 'I don't want to accept anyone's charity, Matt.'

He nodded very slightly, as though he was quite capable of understanding the basis for what must seem like very stubborn pride on her part. But he didn't understand, thought Daisy. The reason for her not wanting to go and live somewhere else was nothing to do with not wanting to accept charity from Matt. It was much simpler than that.

She wanted to stay because she loved him and because she thought that if she stayed then the odds were stacked in her favour. That he might begin to care for her too.

'So that's your final word on the subject, is it, Daisy?'

'Yes.'

'Well, if that's the case, then we'd better get a few things straight from the beginning.'

'What kind of things?'

'Well, for one thing, I do *not* want to see you strolling round the flat in your bra and knickers—'

'Don't you, Matt?' she queried sweetly, but he gave her such a look that she immediately shut up.

'No provocative behaviour; do you understand?'

'Yes, Matt.'

'And if I discover that you aren't putting one hundred and ten per cent into getting top grades in your exams I'll throw you out on your ear and I won't give a stuff what happens to you. This is your last chance not to mess up your future—do you understand *that*?'

'Yes, Matt,' she repeated. 'Any other cheery words of encouragement?'

The grey eyes glittered ominously. 'We ought to discuss the hours I'll expect from you.' He gave her a steady stare. 'I'll only be going into the office half-time. I'll be here in the mornings, while you go off to your tutorial—by the way, I've arranged for you to be taught by an old friend of mine.'

Just like that, thought Daisy.

'In the afternoons,' he continued, 'I'd like you to take over from me and look after Sophie.'

Which meant she got to spend every evening with him! 'That sounds fine,' put in Daisy quickly. It sounded like bliss!

'And occasionally, of course, I'd like you to babysit.'

Daisy felt as though someone had dropped a heavy weight onto the top of her head from a very high building. 'B-babysit?'

'That's right.'

'In the—evenings?'

He raised his eyebrows. 'Of course in the evenings; not every evening, of course. I'm not that much of a slave-driver. You don't have any objections, do you?'

'No. Of course not. For business dinners, I suppose? That kind of thing?'

He gave her a mocking look as comprehension dawned in his eyes. 'That depends. I'm not going to have to gain your permission every time I go out with a woman, am I, Daisy?'

A *woman*?

There was one brief and mad and totally frightening moment when Daisy actually felt like punching him on the jaw. But a jaw like Matt's was impenetrable. Somehow, she managed to keep the smile on her face.

'Of course not, Matt. Just as long as the same rule applics to me.'

The flicker of irritation in the grey eyes was unmistakable. 'Certainly,' he said. 'Though I'm relying on you to exercise caution and common sense in deciding who you bring back here.'

'You're going to vet them all, I suppose?'

'I might,' he said heavily. 'And I shall certainly consider your moral welfare to be my responsibility while you're here.'

'And what's *that* supposed to mean?'

'You know exactly what it means, Daisy,' he answered silkily. 'But just in case you're in any doubt I'll spell it out for you. *There will definitely be no men staying here.* You might be going all out to get rid of your virginity—but you won't be doing it *here*! It is *my* home, after all, and you are *my* responsibility.'

Daisy glared at him, her hackles rising with indignation at his insulting stupidity. How could he believe she'd even *look* at another man? 'And what about *you*?' she demanded. 'Are there exactly the same rules for you? Or will you be bringing hordes of women home to spend the night with you?'

He gave her a hard, bright look. 'No. I have my daughter to consider.' He glanced at his watch. 'And now that we've thrashed all that out satisfactorily, do you still like Chinese food?'

'Yes,' said Daisy, wondering why her future seemed to stretch out in front of her with all the allure of a queue at an execution. 'Why?'

'I thought I'd order some for supper. Then I must go and do some work.'

While Daisy was unpacking, the food arrived. It was undoubtedly the best Chinese meal she'd ever tasted, but it was wasted on Daisy. She unenthusiastically prodded at the rapidly cooling noodles on her plate, unable to shake off a distinct feeling of disappointment.

Because she had the strongest suspicion that living with Matt was not going to resemble any of her wildest fantasies. Not in the slightest.

CHAPTER EIGHT

DAISY was right; living with Matt was *nothing* like
she'd thought it would be, although it was certainly
an education.

She found that after her break from studying she
had to work really hard in order to catch up with
the subjects she'd dropped, but Danny, the middle-
aged Irish tutor Matt had hired for her, was a superbly enthusiastic teacher. And a hard taskmaster.

'Sure, it's more than my job's worth to let you
get away with anything other than straight As,' he
joked one day. 'Matt's paying me a fortune, after
all.'

He used Matt's name easily.

'Do you know him well?' asked Daisy curiously.

'Matt?' Danny nodded. 'Sure I do. Met him at
Cambridge—I taught him, actually. Best student I
ever had.'

Typical! He *would* be, thought Daisy grimly.
'And what made you decide to leave Cambridge?'

He shrugged. 'I hated the academic life—dull as
ditchwater—and when Matt offered me a job I
jumped at it.'

Daisy's eyes widened. 'You mean you actually
work for Matt?'

'Sure I do! I'm his financial advisor which is a
fancy name for doing a bit of creative book-
keeping. But I'm on sabbatical at the moment and
supposed to be getting you through your exams, so

will you quit your chattering, Daisy, and answer that question I've set you?'

Daisy also discovered that daily exposure to Sophie rendered the child even more enchanting than she had imagined; it crept up on her quite gently, and she wasn't sure exactly when it happened, but one day she realised that she had grown to love Matt's baby.

And Sophie's father? Well, nothing had changed there. Daily exposure to Matt didn't make her tire of him, or grow bored by him. Quite the opposite, in fact. Exposure to Matt made Daisy realise that she would never love any other man in quite the same way that she loved him.

Not that he exactly encouraged contact between them; indeed, Daisy hadn't been exaggerating when she'd accused him of leaving the room as soon as she entered. He seemed happiest when he was apart from her; but she wasn't stupid. She knew exactly why he was avoiding her.

He still wanted her.

She could see it in the small sideways glances he threw at her when he thought she wasn't looking. She could tell by the way his eyes lingered reluctantly on her body. And she could feel it in the tension which buzzed in the air when Sophie was in bed and they were alone in the sitting room—and *that*, she knew, was why he tried to avoid her as much as possible.

But it was inevitable that they should spend some time together, especially with the baby, and for Daisy these were the best times of all. Because when Sophie was with them the barriers which he always seemed to erect came tumbling down. He was vis-

ibly softer and more relaxed, and time after time
Daisy found herself staring at his long-legged frame
wistfully, wishing that he wouldn't keep pushing
her away, that he would take her in his arms again
and kiss her like there was no tomorrow.

No such luck, she thought with resignation one
Sunday evening when he was driving them back
from Hamilton Hall, where they'd just spent the
weekend. Daisy's sister Poppy had been visiting
with her new baby and Daisy had felt like quite an
expert in comparison. She'd been really buoyed up
by Matt's glances when Poppy had asked for *her*
advice on what solid foods were best suited to
babies.

And then her world came crashing down about
her ears, because the following day she learnt the
true extent of Matt's involvement with his
assistant...

Daisy was eating cold baked beans from out of
the tin that evening when Matt strolled into the
kitchen, doing up one of his cuff-links. It was little
things like that which brought the sham intimacy
of their living together slamming home. He winced
slightly when he saw what she was eating.

'Is that a good idea?' he murmured.

Daisy spooned another mouthful in unrepentantly. 'It's a brilliant idea—reminds me of when I
used to go away to Brownie camp.' She eyed his
outfit. 'Be careful I don't spatter tomato sauce all
over your suit!' she joked, teasingly holding the tin
up in the air in front of him.

He was dressed in an immaculate black dinner
jacket with a snowy shirt and a neat black silk bow-
tie. His hair was still very slightly damp from the

shower. Suddenly the baked beans lost all their allure and Daisy put the tin down on the work surface.

'Are you going out?' she asked, desperately trying to sound casual.

His grey eyes were mocking. 'No, Daisy—I just thought I'd dress up like this to lounge around the apartment watching television!' Then he saw her mulish expression and his face softened. 'Yes, actually I am. I'm having an early supper, then going on to the opera afterwards.'

'That sounds nice.'

'I'm sure it will be,' he answered blandly. 'And what about you? How are *you* planning to entertain yourself this evening?'

She viciously ground some pepper out of the mill onto half a tomato. 'Oh, I dare say I could go out with one of the *hundreds* of people I happen to know in London!' she fumed sarcastically.

'There's no need to make yourself sound like Little Orphan Annie—Danny said that he'd make sure that you met some other students,' he said carefully.

'He has, and they're all under twenty—I don't seem to have a thing in common with them! They all seem so young!'

'Daisy, you *are* only eighteen yourself,' Matt pointed out.

'A very *mature* eighteen-year-old.' Who, incidentally, would *love* to be taken to the opera, she added silently.

'I know, I know,' he said, slightly grimly.

'Anyway,' she said moodily, 'even if I did have anything in common with them I couldn't possibly

go out. There's Sophie to consider. Besides which,
I've never been set so much work in my life. Danny
is an absolute slave-driver.'

'Good,' said Matt neutrally, but there was a brief
flash of satisfaction in the cool grey eyes. 'I'm glad
that Sophie comes first with you, and as for
Danny—that's what he's there for.' He fastened the
other elegant gold cuff-link and gave her a half-
smile. 'Well, goodnight, Daisy. I expect you'll be
asleep by the time I get home.'

He turned to leave, and her heart contracted at
the sight of those gorgeous broad shoulders; she
found herself remembering when she'd felt them
beneath her fingertips, and how she'd marvelled at
the thrust of raw, masculine power as he'd en-
folded her in his arms.

'Who are you going with?' she asked him
suddenly.

He stopped. 'With a friend,' he said, in an odd
kind of voice.

She was only asking him what *any* flatmate would
ask him, she told herself. 'Anyone I know?' she
persisted, knowing damned well that he hadn't
brought any of his friends back in all the time she'd
been living there.

He shook his head. 'No.'

'Is it a woman?'

He gave her a long, cool look. 'Yes,' he answered
calmly.

'Your girlfriend?'

He sighed. 'Barbara is twenty-six.'

Barbara. So the enemy even had a name, and
one which rang a bell. The woman who had decor-

ated his flat. Who 'knows my taste'. Barbara. His assistant.

'You mean she isn't your girlfriend?'

'I was about to say that, given her age, she's hardly a girl.' He raised his dark brows in enigmatic query. 'But if you're asking me whether I'm having a relationship with her—'

'Yes, I am,' said Daisy boldly, holding her breath as she waited for the guillotine to fall. 'Are you?'

'What do you think?' he countered coolly, and Daisy felt a brief, murderous rage as he glanced down at his wristwatch. 'And now I really must be going. Goodnight, Daisy.'

'Goodnight, Matt,' she answered automatically.

She stood and watched him as he walked away, and then threw the beans down the waste-disposal unit.

She lay awake waiting for his return, and when she heard him quitely moving around the apartment she reached out for the luminous face of her watch. It was almost four-thirty. And, while Daisy might be hopeful and naïve, she wasn't stupid enough to imagine that Matt had been sitting drinking coffee with Barbara until that time in the morning.

She brooded about it all next morning at her tutorial, unable to concentrate on her work, so that Danny bit her head off on more than one occasion. She was so busy wondering if Barbara was very beautiful—she would be, of course—that she dawdled on the way home and was late to take over from Matt.

She was breathless when she burst into the apartment to find him dressed for the office, sitting on the floor building a skyscraper out of Lego for Sophie, who looked up and shrieked, 'Day-zee!'

'Hello, darling.' She grinned at her small charge, then looked at Matt, trying to tell from his expression whether he'd had a night of hot sex. She couldn't. 'Sorry I'm late.'

He shook his head. 'That's OK. It's no hardship for me to play with Sophie for an extra half an hour.'

'But now *you'll* be late for work.'

He gave her a faint smile as he kissed his daughter goodbye and headed for the door. 'Well, I *am* the boss. It's one of the perks.'

'And you *did* have a late night,' she put in slyly.

He ignored that, merely asked, 'What are you planning to do this afternoon?'

She looked out of the huge picture window; cotton-wool clouds were drifting around a spring sky which was as blue as the Swedish flag. 'It's such a glorious day, I thought I'd take Sophie for a walk in the park. Feed the ducks.'

'That sounds nice.'

For a minute there he'd sounded almost envious. 'Why don't you come with us? Sophie would love it.'

He smiled. 'What? Take the afternoon off and play hookey?'

'Well, you *are* the boss—you just said so.'

'And I also have a company to run.' He ruffled Sophie's hair. 'Bye.'

Daisy walked the buggy through Hyde Park at what seemed like a hundred miles an hour, but no amount of brisk exercise seemed able to rid her of the hopelessness which had suddenly overtaken her.

Why can't I just accept that he isn't interested in me? she wondered desperately as she stopped to change the buggy into the lying position, since Sophie had fallen fast asleep. That the 'attraction' he talked about was short-lived and now he's found someone else?

Or maybe he'd had her all along...

Her footsteps slowed as she realised that she had walked almost to the street where Matt's London headquarters were housed. What an amazing sense of direction I have, she thought sardonically, especially since I've only ever visited once before.

That had been in the early days when she'd first moved in with Matt. He had asked her to bring some papers in, and she had excitedly obliged, then been completely overwhelmed by the evidence of his obvious success. And that time, according to Matt, Barbara had been on holiday.

Perhaps if I could just *see* her, thought Daisy. Just once. If I met her and spoke to her, even saw her and Matt together as a couple, then maybe it would help me to realise that Barbara isn't just a name I heard him use—she's the person who's sharing Matt's life. And Matt's bed, most probably.

Making her mind up, she resolutely walked towards Chalcott Street.

Matt's offices were housed in three beautiful mews cottages which stood next to each other, and were linked by a series of interconnecting doors. She remembered him telling her on one of their trips to the park that he hated modern, glass-fronted skyscrapers which blemished the landscape; he liked beautifully constructed old buildings.

She rang the bell and asked to see him, but a disembodied voice from the entry-phone told her that he was out.

This was better than she had hoped for. 'Then could I see Barbara, his assistant, for a moment, please?'

'May I ask who's speaking?'

'It's Daisy. Daisy Blair.'

Minutes later, Daisy was wheeling the buggy into a bright, airy room at the back of the middle house, and the woman who was sitting behind the desk rose gracefully to her feet to greet her.

As soon as she walked into the office, Daisy's heart sank; she was aware that her long hair was tangled after her walk, her jeans all grass-stained at the knees from playing with Sophie, and that she wasn't wearing a scrap of make-up. And that the woman in front of her couldn't have been more different. Barbara wore an elegantly tailored dress of dove-grey linen, with not a single crease in sight. She had an icy Nordic beauty, with naturally blonde hair which was swept back into a chignon and the rare, faintly olive complexion which sometimes accompanies fair hair.

'Hello, Daisy,' she said warmly in a faint but distinctive Transatlantic accent, and held her hand out. 'I'm Barbara Maddox. We haven't actually met, but Matt's always singing your praises—so I half feel I know you! I'm afraid that you've called at rather a bad time, because he's out and won't be back inside the hour.' She gave a faint frown. 'He didn't actually mention that he was expecting you—'

'He wasn't,' said Daisy hastily. 'But I was just passing, and so I thought I'd call in. On the off chance,' she finished lamely.

'Well, now that you're here, and as Sophie seems to be lost to the world—' she nodded at Sophie, who was fast asleep and noisily sucking her thumb '—would you like some coffee?'

A percolator was bubbling temptingly on a table in the corner of the room, and Daisy was curious to find out more about the woman. 'Yes, please. I'd love some.'

'Then do sit down.'

Daisy slid onto a leather sofa which stood in front of a gleaming table. Glass bowls of blowsy roses were dotted around the place, filling the room with their heavenly scent. It looked, thought Daisy, more like a very elegant drawing room than the London headquarters of an international property company.

Barbara Maddox poured the coffee, then put the two china cups on the table and sat down opposite Daisy.

'Thank you,' said Daisy, very politely, and then, more for something to say than anything else, asked, 'You're American?'

Barbara shook her perfectly coiffed blonde head. 'I'm English, as it happens, but I've worked in the States with Matt for quite a long while—only *I* seem to have picked up the accent and he doesn't!'

'Oh,' said Daisy, frowning slightly. 'I see.' But something was troubling her. The woman in front of her was implying that the relationship had been a long-standing one, but how could it have been when up until some ten months ago he had still been married to Patti? Unless the romantic side of their relationship had only flourished after Patti's death?

Barbara Maddox elegantly crossed one beautifully shaped and silk-clad leg over the other. 'So. Matt tells me that Sophie adores you, that you're absolutely wonderful with babies.'

'Well, Sophie's easy to be wonderful with and— Oh!' Daisy exclaimed without thinking, her eyes drawn to the discreet gleam of gold on Barbara Maddox's finger. 'You—I mean—you're married!'

Barbara shook her head. 'Well, actually, no. Not any more. I was widowed several years ago.'

Daisy could have bitten her tongue off. She clapped her hand over her mouth in horror. 'Oh, heavens, I didn't mean—'

The older woman shook her head again. 'Please don't apologise. It's a natural mistake to make. I wear the ring partly out of habit, partly to discourage those men who think that widows are rather easy game and partly because my husband still seems so very real to me. I should take it off, but I can't somehow bring myself to do so.

'And you, my dear,' she said with sudden perceptiveness as she stared at Daisy's pink cheeks, 'are in love with Matt.'

Daisy flushed to the roots of her golden-brown hair. 'Is it that obvious?'

Barbara Maddox gave her an understanding smile. 'It is to me, but then I'm better at recognising it than most. I've known Matt a long time, remember.'

'Please don't tell him!' Daisy beseeched.

'Don't you think he already knows?' asked the older woman gently. 'Matt's one of the most perceptive men I've ever met. And he's certainly no stranger to women falling in love with him, you know.'

Which seemed to make it a million times worse for Daisy—thinking that she was merely one in a cast of thousands. 'I should never have come here—'

'Just why *did* you come here?'

Daisy looked into the other woman's kind eyes and knew that she couldn't tell a lie. 'I wanted to see what you looked like.'

'I don't think I understand.'

'I thought that if I could just *see* you, then you'd become more real, and then I'd be able to accept that Matt was in love with you, and to stop harbouring any foolish hopes myself.'

Barbara frowned. 'Matt isn't in love with me.'

Daisy swallowed. 'But you're seeing him?'

'He takes me out occasionally and it's always most enjoyable—but then Matt is perfect company, as I'm sure you know. However, I get the distinct feeling that just lately Matt has become very fond of using diversionary tactics to get him out of the house.' She looked at Daisy questioningly. 'And perhaps that has something to do with you?'

Daisy shook her head. 'I don't think so.'

'Don't you?' Barbara Maddox took a thoughtful sip of her coffee. 'Matt was a very good friend of my late husband,' she said suddenly. 'They met in New York just after Matt graduated. He was best man at our wedding. I never worked all through our married life; we were waiting for the . . . babies to come along, but they never did. And then Charles died very suddenly. We'd never got around to taking out life assurance. When you're young it isn't something you really think of. And I'd never trained for anything.'

She paused and her eyes were very soft. 'So financially, as well as emotionally, I was in a right old mess, and Matt gave me a job, even though I was ridiculously underqualified for it. But he believed in me—and he's a very good friend to people he believes in.'

'I know,' said Daisy. 'He's helping me right now.'

'The thing about Matt,' said Barbara Maddox, 'and you probably think I'm being frightfully indiscreet in telling you this, but somehow in this instance I don't think it matters—the thing about Matt is that his time with Patti has made him cynical about relationships. It was no secret in New York that the relationship was unhappy but he never talks about it, and I never ask him.'

Daisy's eyes widened, and she put her coffee-cup down. Just *how* unhappy? she wondered.

Barbara Maddox frowned. 'I think he's trying to lock the emotional side of himself away, to concentrate exclusively on looking after Sophie, and I think that would be a dreadful shame. I think there's a lot of untapped emotion in Matt that's just waiting to be set free.'

'And I want to be the one to do it,' said Daisy huskily, speaking her thoughts aloud.

'Well, why shouldn't you be?'

'Because I'm a woman, for one thing. And we're taught that it's the man who should do the running ...'

At this Barbara Maddox threw her head back and roared with laughter. 'My dear, women have been chasing men since the beginning of time and anyone who denies that is a liar. The secret is to let them believe that they are the ones doing the chasing! I think that Matt is very fond of you, but he's fighting it for all kinds of reasons.'

Daisy walked back to the apartment with her heart singing at everything Barbara Maddox had said. Bless the woman! He *wasn't* in love with his assistant! Which left the way wide open for Daisy.

What was it they said—nothing ventured, nothing gained? And Matt had spoken about returning to the States in August. She had to do something before then.

Because, rightly or wrongly, she intended to seduce Matt Hamilton, to make him realise that there was one woman for him, and her name was Daisy Blair...

CHAPTER NINE

'OH, MATT—*please*!'

Matt laughed. 'Daisy, you can't go out and celebrate your exams on the night you've taken them. There are two whole months to wait for the results. What if you've failed them?'

'I won't have failed them,' said Daisy smugly. The papers had been a breeze, and she really felt as though she had given them her all. 'I'm willing to bet you any money you like that I'll get absolutely wonderful grades.'

He shook his dark head in mock reprimand. 'I am not a gambling man. And you know what they say pride comes before.'

'There'll be no fall, Matt, I can assure you,' she said with cool confidence.

He sighed, but the smoky grey eyes were glimmering with amusement. 'OK, I'll take you out for dinner, Daisy. Your enthusiasm is too infectious to resist. But who are we going to find to look after Sophie?'

Daisy shook her head. 'No one. Let's go early and take her with us.'

'Where did you have in mind?'

'There's a new pizza and burger bar open in Kensington.'

'I can see that you don't intend to burn a huge hole in my pocket,' he observed wryly. 'But you can be as extravagant as you like; I *can* afford it.'

'No,' she told him firmly. She *wanted* to take Sophie with them. She didn't want to sit in some stuffy restaurant with waiters gliding over with giant pepper-pots every time there was a lull in the conversation. 'It's the perfect place. They even have clowns to entertain the children—'

'Well, that should keep you both amused,' he commented drily, but Daisy ignored the remark. She wasn't going to rise to it. Later tonight she intended to show Matt Hamilton that she was all woman!

The evening went perfectly. They were seated in the restaurant at six o'clock and had their order taken, whereupon Sophie immediately proceeded to smear garlic bread all over her face.

'And to drink?' queried Matt, looking at Daisy over the top of his menu.

He could be so stuffy about her drinking alcohol. He could be stuffy full stop. 'Red wine?' she enquired hopefully.

'Shouldn't it be champagne?' he questioned with some amusement. 'If you're so certain that we've something to celebrate?'

'Oh, I'd absolutely love champagne!'

'Champagne it is, then.' He smiled at the waitress as he handed her the menu and Daisy jealously watched the voluptuous redhead who was all over him like a rash.

She sighed as she peeped at him surreptitiously from beneath her lashes. Not that she could blame the waitress—he looked good enough to eat tonight, wearing beautifully cut linen trousers and a midnight-blue raw silk shirt. Scrumptious, thought

Daisy, acutely aware of the powerful thighs just inches away from her knees.

A few minutes later Matt leaned back in his chair and watched her sip her champagne, the bubbles going up her nose so that she jumped a little, like a cat accidentally bursting a bubble, and he found his mouth softening. 'So tell me what your plans are when you get your results.'

She didn't dare! If he knew what her plans were, he would probably high-tail it out of the restaurant! Daisy struggled for composure, but already the unaccustomed champagne was making her feel a little giddy, and the anticipation of what she intended to do was making the blood fizz hotly along her veins. She took a deep breath.

'You mean after you've gone back to the States?' she asked him sweetly.

'That's right.'

What would he say if he knew that she was planning on going to the States with him? 'I definitely don't want to go through college.'

'Oh? Why not?'

She grimaced. 'Much too time-consuming. I'd like to go straight out to work.'

'Just like that?'

'Just like that,' she smiled.

'I suppose you know just what kind of work that will be?' he queried sardonically.

'Actually, yes.' She nodded earnestly. 'I'm going to go into advertising. Copy-writing, preferably.'

'You've chosen a notoriously competitive field!' he observed.

'I know.'

He took a sip of his own drink and observed her through his dark lashes. 'So what makes you think you'd excel at writing clever slogans for advertising campaigns?'

'I think on my feet, and I'm good with words,' she said breezily.

'And so modest to boot,' he murmured.

'The modern woman doesn't hide her assets away,' said Daisy firmly.

'No,' agreed Matt, and she watched his eyes darken as they swept reluctantly over her.

Triumph washed over her as she saw a blaze of desire heating the normally cool grey eyes. No one could have been more demurely dressed than Daisy was this evening—in an ankle-length printed grunge dress and clumpy black shoes—but Matt was far from impervious to her; she could tell that much from the two flares of colour which emphasised the aristocratically high cheekbones.

'Tell me what else modern women do,' he said, interrupting her reverie with a husky voice.

She looked at him suspiciously, suspecting sarcasm, but his face remained deadpan. 'They assert themselves, Matt. They decide what they want out of life and then they go for it.' And *how*! she thought.

'Do they, now?'

There was a slightly fraught silence as they looked at one another, broken only by Daisy saying, 'Matt? Could you please call the waitress over? Sophie's just up-ended the sugar bowl.'

Matt put Sophie to bed when they got back to the apartment, and when he walked back into the sitting room he found Daisy slotting a compact disc into the player. He frowned. 'Now what are you doing?'

She kicked her clumpy black shoes off and started jiggling around in time to the music. 'Don't be so dense, Matt! What does it look like? I'm playing us some music. I want to dance!'

The frown increased. 'What for?'

If only he knew! 'What do people usually dance for? It's fun, that's why!'

'I have no desire to dance,' he said repressively.

'Well, how about having a nightcap together?'

His face darkened. 'I do *not*,' he said deliberately, in his most pompous voice, 'want a nightcap either. And neither do you—you drank most of the champagne at the restaurant. *No*, Daisy!' he added sternly. 'No amount of wide-eyed pleading will change my mind. It's been a wonderful evening, but it's over. And now I'm going to shower and get to bed. I'll see you tomorrow.'

For a moment she felt deflated as she watched him leave. So much for the soft lights and music! Things never worked out the way you thought they were going to, she thought gloomily.

But within moments her usual spirit had returned, and she crept along the corridor until she stood outside Matt's door. She heard the sound of the *en suite* bathroom door being opened, and the faint hiss of water being turned on.

Her heart was pounding as she silently pushed down the door handle and went inside. Then she took off her dress, her bra and her knickers, and hid them in one of his drawers. The room was illuminated only by a soft peachy pool of light from the bedside lamp, and Daisy pulled the covers back and climbed into Matt's bed.

Beneath the cool sheets she lay throbbing with excitement as she waited for what seemed like hours. She was beginning to wonder if he'd actually drowned in there when she heard the water jets cease their hissing sound, and she slid further down the bed, suddenly quaking with nerves at what she was about to do.

He clicked the bathroom light off and walked into the room, rubbing a white towel into the damp darkness of his hair, another tiny white towel, which barely covered him, knotted at his hips...

Daisy's mouth went bone-dry as she saw all that wonderful bare flesh on show, her eyes feasting on his magnificent body. Somewhat awesomely, she observed the tiny droplets of water which sparkled all over that exquisitely tanned and hair-roughened torso, and the sleek, rippling power of his upper arms. And if you added to all that the long, muscular legs which seemed to go on for ever, well... Matt was the most perfect man she could have imagined in her wildest dreams.

She thought that she gave a little gasp. She must have uttered something, for he froze, staring down at the bed as if he couldn't believe what he was seeing.

His eyes narrowed. A muscle began to work furiously in his cheek. For a moment he seemed to find it impossible to say anything and when he did finally manage to speak it was to say exactly what Daisy had been expecting him to say. Or something pretty close to it.

'Just what do you think you're playing at?' he queried in a voice of dangerous silk.

She was clever with words, but words wouldn't do. It was no good trying to reason with him. She had to appeal to something far more fundamental in Matt's nature than reason. She wanted to touch his heart, but in order to do that...

Without saying anything, she sat up in bed, the sheets falling in alabaster folds around her slender waist. She shook her head slightly, so that the golden-brown strands of her hair streamed like satin over her tip-tilted breasts, her pose illuminated by the peachy light from the lamp.

She saw his eyes darken, heard the hiss as he dragged air unsteadily into his lungs. She saw the effort of will it took for him to stare unblinkingly into her face. 'Get—*out*,' he said falteringly.

'Matt—'

'Get out of here, Daisy,' he repeated. 'Or you may get more than you bargained for.'

She curved her lips into a smile at that, and saw the answering flash of desire in his eyes.

His eyes never leaving her face, he threw the towel he was holding onto the floor, then his hand went to the knot of the other one which was tied so carelessly at one narrow hip.

Daisy's heart sounded very loud in her ears.

'OK, Daisy. If you want to play games, we'll play games. I'm going to count to five, and if you're not out of here by then I'm going to get into that bed and make love to you all night long because it's been a very long time since I made love to anyone and you are very, very beautiful. But I'm going to be damned angry about it. Do you understand?'

She sat there silently, hypnotised by the sight of him.

'One...'

She swallowed as he began to unwork the knot.

'Two...'

Her heart was racing like a train as she watched the deft movement of his fingers.

'Three...'

Her breasts tightened in anticipation and she saw from the tortured look on his face that the fact had not escaped him either.

'Four... I'm warning you, Daisy...' he said, in a kind of desperate voice.

She felt a warm, moist excitement pooling at the fork of her body.

'This is your last chance...' But it came out as a strangely husky entreaty.

There was a deafening silence.

'Five...'

And now it was too late to object—not that she had the slightest intention of objecting—because the knot was no more and the towel had fluttered to the floor and he stood there, silent and arrogantly proud in all his nakedness, and Daisy blushed as she saw how magnificently aroused he was.

'Oh, yes,' he affirmed softly as he saw in which shocked and amazed direction her eyes had swerved. 'See what you've done to me? Does that daunt you, Daisy?'

'No,' she said breathlessly.

'And this. Does this daunt you?' And she watched with a pounding heart as he bent and reached into the bedside locker for a small foil package which he slowly began to unwrap. She knew what it was, of course. She'd never seen one before, but she knew exactly what it was. His gaze captured hers hypnotically as he slowly stroked the condom on, over the hard, swollen length of his arousal. 'Does it?' he repeated softly.

'N-no.'

'It should.'

She couldn't speak as he moved towards the bed and climbed in beside her, something unfathomable in his eyes as he smoothed back the hair from her head with a hand which was almost gentle, and when he spoke it was with a reluctant unsteadiness which melted her heart.

'It isn't too late, Daisy, not quite. I still have some small part of me which will respond to common sense, but not for much longer—so please go, sweetheart; go *now*.'

For an answer she put her arms around his neck and kissed him, rapturously pressing her naked breasts into his chest, hearing his little moan of surrender as he buried his hands into the rich silkiness of her hair. He plundered her mouth like some sweet, marauding pirate and she opened her mouth wide to him, releasing all the pent-up passion she'd been longing to give him for so long. It was some kiss.

'Hell!' he gasped.

His hands moved down to explore her skin eagerly, those slightly roughened fingertips touching every single inch of her until she felt that there was not a bit of her he hadn't caressed.

But she was wrong.

When his hand reached down to alight with delicate precision on that most intimate part of her she shuddered with helpless longing.

'Matt!' she gasped against his mouth.

'Do you like it?' he murmured.

'Oh, God,' she whispered. 'Yes. *Yes!* Matt! Oh, please, Matt,' she moaned.

As his finger lightly circled, she said his name over and over again, as though she couldn't believe that it was actually him in her arms, and through the kiss he instructed her with husky command, 'Now touch me, Daisy. Touch me too.'

She wasn't in the least bit shy or intimidated as her slender hand half encircled the throbbing hardness of him, exploring this totally alien part of him with rapt preoccupation, experimenting with the touch of her fingertips, the gentle caressing slide of her palm against the hard, satiny skin.

'Like that?'

'Yes,' he rasped. '*Just* like that!'

She felt him shudder against her as she began to stroke delicate fingers up and down in some instinctive rhythm, and was astonished when he abruptly stopped kissing her and brutally snatched her hand away from him.

'That's enough,' he ordered breathlessly.

'Enough?' For a minute she was terrified that he was going to stop and kick her out of his bedroom.

He must have read the fear in her eyes, for he gave a strange kind of laugh. 'Oh, no, Daisy,' he said softly. 'I'm certainly not going to stop. Do you really think I could stop now, when I've wanted to do this for so long?' There was an edge to his voice, a desperation and something else, too... Recrimination? Daisy wondered; but she immediately blocked the thought away, her body melting with relieved and honeyed longing as he again began to stroke delicate little circles at the very deepest core of her.

'Just take it easy,' he urged her, his mouth licking provocatively at her breast, and she felt the nipple ruck against the slow slide of his tongue. 'Touch me like that again and it will be all over too quickly—much too quickly for you. And I don't want it to be over. I want to do it to you all night. Oh, God, Daisy—you're so wet. You're so ready and beautiful, and I don't want to hurt you.'

But his hands were gently parting her legs as he spoke and Daisy arched eagerly towards him. If there had to be pain, then so be it; she didn't care. For there could be no worse pain than not having Matt do this to her.

'Please,' she whispered. 'Please don't stop.'

He gave a sultry little laugh as he felt her move restlessly against his hand. 'Oh, I won't stop,' he whispered from above her as he pierced into the very heart of her with his silken shaft. He halted briefly when he felt her tense, but within seconds her body had adjusted to the welcome intrusion. She felt herself tighten around him, heard the soft moan of pleasure he made as she did so, and her acceptance of him was enough to allow him to begin the most slow, seductive rhythm as he thrust into her.

She sensed that he was holding back with a sheer effort of will. Time and time again she seemed very close to something very wonderful, something she didn't dare even to acknowledge, for fear that it was some heartbreaking illusion. And time after time the feeling retreated.

Then suddenly she sensed that there would be no further retreat, that she was poised on some magical brink, and Matt sensed it too.

'Yes, now,' he urged softly. 'Now. Now. *Now.*'

Daisy cried out her pleasure as her body erupted into a series of incredible spasms, each one more spellbinding than the last, and then she felt Matt shudder against her as he mouthed something sweet into her ear, though she was so caught up with holding onto the last traces of her orgasm that she couldn't be sure of what he said.

She knew what she was longing for him to say, but maybe it was too soon. And to hear that he loved her would only be icing on top of the most delicious cake...

Daisy slept the deep sleep of the satiated and was disorientated and distinctly grumpy when Matt shook her awake.

'What time is it?' she mumbled from underneath the rumpled sheet.

'Time to get up,' commanded a bitter voice she scarcely recognised, and Daisy's eyelids flew open to see Matt, wearing nothing but a pair of jeans, standing beside the bed, censure in his grey eyes as they coldly surveyed her.

'Matt?' queried Daisy uncertainly, her eyes flicking to the clock and seeing that it was far too early even to be thinking about getting up. 'But it's only five in the morning!' she protested.

'Quite.'

'But—'

'Just get up and get out of here, will you, Daisy?' he interrupted brutally. 'Did you bring clothes with you, or did you simply parade in here naked?'

Daisy swallowed at the ill-concealed disgust in his voice. 'They're over there,' she said, in a voice which was threatening to crack.

'Where?'

'In there.' She pointed to the drawer.

She watched his mouth twist as he extracted the wispy little bra, the matching knickers and the dress, and threw them down contemptuously on the bed.

'Get them on!' he instructed curtly, and stormed out of the bedroom, leaving her staring in bewilderment after him.

When Daisy had scrambled into her clothes, she rushed into the sitting room to find Matt standing forbiddingly at one of the huge picture windows, staring out, unseeing, at a magnificent dawn which was just beginning to gild the London skyline. At the sound of her footsteps he turned round, and her heart sank into her boots when she saw that his face was still like granite. The nightmare was real.

'Matt, what *is* it?' she demanded in a high voice, but one which was nevertheless miraculously steady.

His mouth curved scornfully. 'You mean apart from the fact that I took your virginity last night?'

'But I *wanted* you to!'

'Oh, yes,' he said cuttingly. 'You made *that* abundantly clear. Dear God! For a virgin you scored remarkably well in the seduction stakes! Tell me—had you been taking lessons?'

She stared at him in confusion. 'B-but I thought it was wonderful,' she stumbled. 'Didn't you?'

'Oh, don't be so bloody naïve!' he exploded. 'Of course it was wonderful! Sex *is* wonderful—why else do you think people make such damned fools of themselves over it?'

'Including you, I suppose?' she asked, in a small voice.

'Yes, including me,' he said bitterly.

She decided to try one last appeal, laying it all on the line, and if *this* didn't move him, then she would know she had lost him. 'But I love you, Matt,' she whispered softly. 'You know I do.'

His mouth straightened. Never had he looked so gorgeous. Or so remote. '*Love?*' he queried in disbelief. 'Well, if that's your idea of love, then it's a particularly manipulative kind of emotion. I should think carefully about calling it that in future. I'd tend to categorise it as playing Lolita myself.'

Daisy's temper, which had begun to simmer when he'd kicked her out of bed, now threatened to boil over. 'Lolita?' she questioned hotly. 'I'm no Lolita! Will you get it into your thick skull that I'm *years* older than Lolita was? And what about you?'

'What *about* me?' he snarled.

'You've enjoyed strutting around playing Pygmalion with *me*, haven't you? "Daisy, you will do this!" and "Daisy, you will do that!" Moving me around as though I was a chess piece!'

'Don't try to be smart!'

'I can't help it—I *am* smart!'

'Not smart enough,' Matt said grimly, 'if you think that seducing me is about to win you a proposal of marriage.'

'*Win* you?' Daisy yelled in disbelief. 'You see yourself as some sort of competition prize, do you? Well, so do I—the booby prize!'

He glared right back at her and there was a silence in which the only sound which could be heard was their angry breathing. And then he dropped his bombshell. 'That's it!' he said decisively. 'I'm going back to the States, Daisy.'

She forced herself to stay calm, even though her heart was racing with fear. 'When?'

'As soon as it can be arranged.'

'And how soon is that?'

'This afternoon, I hope.'

'So soon, Matt?' she mocked. 'And what about Sophie? Who's going to look after her?'

'I'll manage,' he said shortly.

'What about me?' she asked slowly, reluctantly.

'There's no problem there. I own this apartment. You are, of course, welcome to stay here for as long as you like—'

'I wouldn't stay here if—'

'And before you rashly commit yourself to any course of action which could seriously affect your future,' he put in coldly, 'I would advise you to hear me out. You are welcome to stay here for as long as you like. Your alternative is to return to Hamilton Hall, but since you intend to work in the world of advertising I don't imagine that it would be a very good idea to be living in the middle of the countryside.'

He gestured to a piece of paper which lay on one of the tables, and Daisy detected a slight awkwardness in the movement. 'I've left a cheque.'

'For services rendered?'

'That's enough!' His mouth twisted. 'By terminating your employment so abruptly, I obviously owe you at least a month's salary in lieu of notice. Please pay it into your account, and there is more money available—'

'I wouldn't touch your money if—'

'Spare me the clichéd melodramatics, Daisy,' he interrupted cuttingly. He lifted a dark brow. 'You need to eat.'

She tried one last time. 'So that's it, is it, Matt? Over?'

He stuffed his hands into the pockets of his jeans, stretching the fabric indecently across the muscular shafts of his thighs, and nodded. 'I'm afraid it's the only way, Daisy.'

'I see.' It was odd, thought Daisy, how in the space of a few short hours you could veer from elation to complete despair.

'I wish you well in your chosen future,' he said heavily. 'And I think it's probably best for everyone concerned if you go out for the day while I'm packing, don't you?'

'Before I do,' she said, in a voice which she couldn't prevent wobbling, 'I want to say— g-goodbye. To Sophie.'

For the first time, his arrogant poise seemed to waver. His eyes narrowed, then he nodded. 'But of course,' he said, as formally as he would have to a car-park attendant. 'She'll be awake in an hour.'

CHAPTER TEN

'THERE'S a gentleman out here, Daisy. To see you.'

'What?' Daisy paused, mid-doodle on the large piece of paper in front of her, her mind still caught up with the problem of finding a punchy way to launch a new range of shoe polish to a general public who, it seemed, no longer polished their shoes. She looked down blankly at the intercom on her olympic-swimming-pool-sized desk. 'What?' she queried again absently.

Her secretary sighed as she repeated her statement in the long-suffering voice she always used when Daisy was in one of her 'creative moods'. 'There's a gentleman here to see you, Daisy. Won't give his name.'

'You know I never see anyone without an appointment,' answered Daisy crisply. 'And if it's someone selling something, then tell them I'm not interested.'

'I rather think you might be,' said an amused and horribly familiar voice over the intercom, and Daisy dropped her pencil on the floor in horror. 'Interested, that is.'

'Sir—*please!*' came her secretary's horrified voice. 'You can't do that!'

'I just have,' came the mocking rejoinder, and Daisy buried her head in her hands at the sound of Matt Hamilton's deep, irresistible voice. What the hell was he doing here? And what the hell was she going to do? She glanced nervously up at the door. What if she just told him she didn't want to see him—would that work?

But you're the chief copywriter for one of London's most prestigious advertising agencies, she reminded herself. Assert yourself, woman!

'I don't want to see you, Matt!' she found herself yelling down the intercom. So much for being cool! She had spent the last two years planning how coldly she would react when she saw him again— and here she was, screeching like a parrot!

'So you *do* remember me?' came the deep, smooth voice.

'Of course I remember you!' Daisy exploded. 'No one forgets an arrogant, unfeeling—'

'Daisy, Daisy,' chided the sexiest voice she'd ever encountered, and in the last two years she'd been chatted up by some of the most eligible men in London. 'Your secretary is looking quite shocked and several of your colleagues have begun to gather out here and are listening to the proceedings with a great deal of interest. Now, we *could* continue our conversation like this and regale them as we are at the moment, but I actually think it would do more to maintain your professional reputation if I came in there and we did it in private.'

If only his last words didn't conjure up the most shockingly erotic images, thought Daisy despairingly. 'And if I say no?' she enquired frostily. 'I suppose you'll kick the door down?'

'I wasn't intending to, but I can try.' There was unmistakable laughter in his voice now. 'I really had no idea that such macho techniques turned you on, Daisy.'

That did it! He *would* have her reputation in tatters if she wasn't careful. And hadn't she spent the last two years telling herself over and over again as she'd worked like mad at her career that she no longer gave a damn about Matt Hamilton? Well, now she had the golden opportunity to prove it! 'You'd better come in,' she said resignedly, and the door immediately opened to reveal Matt.

Daisy's mouth dried when she saw him strolling in, wearing white jeans which were disgustingly tight and a white T-shirt which clearly showed just how muscle-packed that magnificent chest was, but still somehow managing to exude the air of a fabulously rich tycoon. How did he do it? She could see her secretary virtually slavering at the mouth. The door closed behind him and he stood watching her.

'Hello, Daisy,' he said softly.

'Hello, Matt,' she answered, and something in her frosty retort seemed to amuse him. She bristled as she subjected him to the same kind of lingering once-over that he was giving *her*.

He was very tanned. Damn him! Where had he been to get a tan like that?

'You're very brown,' she said, without thinking.

'Yeah. It's all over, too.' He grinned. 'Want to see?'

That was just the trouble. She *did*. She wanted to tear every bit of clothing from his body and...and... How she managed not to blush she didn't know, but she silently thanked a benevolent guardian angel.

'What can I do for you, Matt?' she asked coolly, but he was too busy looking around her vast office with its panoramic views to answer.

'I'm impressed,' he said at last. 'Very impressed.'

She wasn't looking for his praise; she didn't need it, either. She knew well enough that she'd succeeded—*and* on her own terms. 'Thanks,' she said drily, but the sarcasm seemed wasted on him, for he smiled and walked over to her desk and sat in the chair in front of her.

'So you made it, Daisy,' he said. 'And how. But then I always knew that you would.'

'Thanks again,' she said testily. 'When I want a testimonial I'll be sure to give your name.'

'Do.' The grey eyes glimmered, and Daisy suddenly realised that he was *here*, flirting with her, and that she was beginning to respond, when she had vowed that if she ever saw the good-for-nothing swine again, then she would tell him exactly what she thought of him. And how much she hated him.

But now she realised that she had been completely fooling herself. And that if she uttered the lie, then it would have the hollow ring of insincerity. And then Matt would know that she was really no different from the brainless little fool who had thrown herself at him and told him she loved him and been kicked out of his bed for her trouble.

And she *was* different.

She was!

'How's Sophie?' She couldn't keep the trace of wistfulness out of her voice. In the early days, she had expected to miss Matt, and she had. Unbearably. It had been like functioning with a limb missing. What she hadn't expected was that she'd miss his daughter quite so much.

'She's gorgeous.' He glanced at his watch. 'In fact, I'm picking her up from nursery in just over an hour.'

'Nursery?' Daisy tried and failed to imagine the chubby baby she'd once known going to nursery.

'Sure. She's three now.'

Daisy knew that. She'd pored over the photos Mrs Hamilton had brought back from her frequent visits to the States, since Matt had not visited England once since that ignominious day two years ago. The day that Matt had told her to get out of his life. Her heart hardened into lead and gave her a new resolve.

She leaned back in her chair, glad that she was wearing her most sophisticated silk trouser suit in a smoky shade of grey. 'So what can I do for you, Matt?' she asked, in the same kind of voice that she would have used to a valued client. It had just the right amount of distance, and she could see a fleeting flash of irritation in his eyes.

Good!

'You can marry me,' he said softly, and Daisy nearly fell off the chair. 'Please.'

There was a stunned silence while the Daisy who was hooked on corny old Hollywood movies and longed to throw herself into his arms and shout, *'When?'* fought with the Daisy who was wise to men, who had the reputation in the advertising world of being a rather tasty but very cool cookie.

The cool cookie won.

She gave him a supercilious look. 'Is this your idea of a joke?'

He shook his dark head. 'No. I've never been more serious in my life. I love you, Daisy. I always have done and I always will.'

'Then you have the most extraordinary way of showing it,' she commented bitterly, unnecessarily rifling through a sheaf of papers so that he shouldn't see how much her hands were shaking. 'Now if you really don't mind I have work to do.' And she stabbed her finger on the documents which were piled up on her desk.

He stood up.

He's leaving, thought Daisy, appalled at the sinking of her heart.

But he wasn't leaving. In fact, at that moment he was striding round to her side of the desk and hauling her to her feet. 'What do you think you're doing?' she demanded hoarsely as she beat her fists angrily and ineffectually against his chest.

'I'm going to save us about three weeks of our lives,' he told her grimly.

'I don't have the slightest idea what you're talking about!'

'Then allow me to enlighten you,' he said, and Daisy recognised the arrogant Matt of old. 'I know that you're angry with me—and you have every right to be—'

'How very good of you!'

'But I don't intend to spend the next month playing games when we both know that you still love me.'

'Why, of all the *arrogant*—'

'And when we both know it would be such a waste of time to be arguing—especially when we could be doing...this...' And he started to kiss her.

He kissed her as she had always dreamed he would kiss her, without restraint or guilt or regret, and when he eventually raised his dark head her mouth was still trembling with the passion of that kiss.

'Why—why did you do that?' she stumbled, and when his arms tightened around her waist she was glad, because she felt weak enough to slide to the ground.

His grey eyes were very clear and very intense. And very determined. 'Perhaps the only way to convince you that I *do* love you is not to tell you but to show you.'

With an effort she pulled away, and he made no attempt to stop her. She shook her head, her golden-brown hair slick and neat in a French plait which hung all the way down her back. 'I'm not the same Daisy,' she told him, 'who loves blindly and foolishly, who believes that she can make someone love her back just because *she* wants it. And I'm all grown-up now, Matt—I don't need a Pygmalion figure to control me. I control my own life now.'

'Good,' he said quietly. 'And I know all of that.'

She turned on him furiously. 'So how can you love me? If I've changed so much, then you don't even *know* me—let alone *love* me!'

But he smiled, and touched her mouth very, very gently with the tip of his finger, tracing the fullness of the curves there so that it trembled again—that wretched, traitorous mouth!

'You have a beautiful heart, Daisy,' he said simply. 'And that will never change. That's why I love you; why I always have loved you; why I had to let you go.'

She shook her head again, swallowing as the memory came back to haunt her. 'Why did you let me go?' she said brokenly, not realising that in her question lay her implicit acceptance of his love; but Matt must have realised it because he closed his eyes briefly.

'I had to let you go for many reasons,' he told her. 'But the main one was that I was aware of how much you loved me.'

So Barbara had been right.

'I knew that long before the night I found you in my bed, and long before you told me you loved me the following morning,' he said. 'I knew that you wanted to marry me and come back and live in the States with me, and be a good mother to Sophie. And don't you think that I wanted that too, Daisy?' he demanded, and there was a catch in his voice.

'You didn't act like a man who wanted it,' she told him hollowly.

'But don't you know *why*? Can't you realise?'

She shook her head in bewilderment.

'Because you were so damned *young*! And, before you start telling me that at eighteen you can legally vote and get married, hear me out first. It wasn't so much your age as your lack of experience. You had so much talent and so much promise and you were about to throw all that away to be with me.'

'But lots of women find fulfilment in marriage and motherhood,' argued Daisy, stung.

'I know they do. But I am also aware, as I'm sure you must be too, that marriage today is a threatened institution; it's difficult to get it to last. Particularly if one of the participants is still in their teens. What if five or ten years down the line you began to regret tying yourself down so early? What if you began to resent me for having the career you'd never had? Or resent Sophie for having the kind of opportunities you'd let slip by?'

She shook her head distractedly. 'I wouldn't have done.'

He took both her hands in his. 'That was a chance I couldn't take. You needed to change, to grow up—as you just said yourself. You needed to explore your talents, and you could only do that on your own. And *I* wanted our marriage to last.'

'And is that what you said to Patti?' she said bitterly, before she could stop herself, voicing the fear which was uppermost in her mind, appalled at the deep vein of jealousy which obviously still ran through her. 'You certainly got over *her* soon enough.'

Matt flinched and then, very determinedly, he lifted her chin so that their eyes were on a collision course.

'I was never married to Patti,' he said, in a dull voice.

Daisy stared at him in disbelief. 'Of course you were married to her! It was in all the papers!'

'And you think that papers only print the truth?' he enquired cynically. 'Our so-called marriage was a story put out by Patti's public relations company, and at Patti's instigation.'

'But why?'

'It's a long story.'

And it was a story she needed to hear. 'Tell me, Matt,' she said firmly.

There was a long pause before he spoke with the air of a man getting rid of a burden he had carried around for much too long. 'As you know, I'd been seeing Patti for several months. It was a pleasant affair, but nothing heavy. She was fun to be with, and I was flattered that she, who could have had any man she wanted, should want me—'

'Spare me the false modesty, Matt,' she interjected drily. 'If we're talking eligible, you'd be up there at the top of the list.'

'I'm pleased you think so.' He gave her the glimmer of a smile. 'From the very start I knew the relationship for what it was—enjoyable but definitely not permanent. I was never in love with Patti and I never wanted to marry her.'

'Did she want to marry you, then?' asked Daisy jealously.

He nodded. 'And once I knew how serious she'd become I planned to end the relationship. But she was so looking forward to seeing my family home that I didn't have the heart not to bring her to the ball as I'd promised. I decided to tell her after that weekend.' He paused. 'And then I walked into the room and saw you standing there, silver ribbons in your hair, wearing that pale blue dress...'

'It was so old-fashioned,' said Daisy, wincing at the memory.

'Yes, it was,' he agreed. 'But that didn't matter. You looked like no one I'd ever seen before. Young and beautiful and innocent. My heart kind of turned over. I found myself unable to keep my eyes off you and yet I kept telling myself, This is *Daisy*, for heaven's sake. But it was confusing—you were still Daisy and yet everything seemed different. Patti guessed, of course. And I was racked with guilt.'

'Why?'

He shrugged his broad shoulders. 'It seemed somehow wrong to want a girl who was barely seventeen the way I wanted you that night. A girl, moreover, I'd grown up with. I tried to tell myself all the reasons why I shouldn't want you, but I couldn't convince myself. When Patti came to my room that night . . .'

'Don't—'

'When Patti came to my room that night . . .' he continued inexorably as he saw her flinch. 'Sweetheart, this is painful for me too—but I have to tell you. It's part of the past which we have to put away, but to do that you must know about it, or it will be like a barrier between us for ever.'

Dumbly, she nodded, her fingernails making tiny little half-moon shapes on the pale skin of her palms.

'Making love to Patti that night had been the last thing on my mind—for reasons which were too complex and too painful for me to acknowledge. And yet on the other hand I was pretty churned up emotionally over what I perceived to be the *wrong* feelings I had for you—a girl who was still so very young.'

He read the question in her eyes and nodded reluctantly. 'Yes, I had sex with Patti that night,' he said baldly. 'When you've been lovers for several months, it isn't difficult. But God forgive me,

Daisy, I did it thinking of *you*, no one but *you*.'

'But you said that you didn't—' It came out as a painful little cry.

'Love her?' he guessed gently, and shook his head. 'And I didn't. But there are more reasons for having sex than being in love, Daisy. Sometimes it can be for comfort, sometimes as a farewell—like that night.' He paused. 'Or so I thought,' he finished, on an almost violent note.

Daisy stared at him uncomprehendingly. 'What do you mean?' she whispered.

'Just that I paid the price for it afterwards.'

Daisy stared at him. 'What price?'

He gave an empty smile. 'Patti wasn't used to men turning her down; she had no intention of letting the relationship finish. She didn't take her pill that night.'

Daisy gasped. 'You mean...?'

'Yes; deliberately. She became pregnant with Sophie. The odds were stacked against it, but she became pregnant, and she wanted marriage.'

'And you didn't?'

He shook his head. 'Of course I didn't. I didn't love her. I loved you, although I still hadn't fully admitted it to myself. I told her that I would stand by her and support her financially and emotionally, but that I could never marry her, that it wouldn't be fair to her or to the baby.'

'Or to you?' said Daisy shrewdly.

'Or to me,' he confirmed. 'Patti thought that I would change my mind. Believe me, she tried every ploy in the book, but I was unmovable. It was then that she played her trump card. When she realised that her emotional blackmail wasn't going to work, she went to the doctor to have the pregnancy terminated, though of course she didn't tell me about it until afterwards.'

Daisy gasped again.

'But by then it was too late,' he said, with a grim kind of satisfaction. 'The pregnancy was too far advanced.'

'So what happened?'

'She told me that she didn't want to bring up a child on her own. She said that if I were to agree to live with her and let her PR people put out a story saying that we were married, then after the baby was born we would have a quick divorce, and she would let me keep the baby...'

A muscle worked furiously in his cheek. 'So we lived together—or rather we led separate lives in the same apartment. We never slept together again after that night. I was terrified that once the baby was born she would change her mind. But thank God she didn't.

'She didn't even want to see Sophie after she'd been born, just handed her over to me and booked herself in at a gym to regain her figure for her next concert tour. She started an affair with her personal trainer soon after that, and then, as you know, a month later she was killed on the tour bus.'

'Poor Patti,' said Daisy suddenly. Not to have wanted her daughter; to have wanted Matt so much that she had deliberately become pregnant. She lifted her hand up and touched Matt's raven hair wonderingly, as though it were the first time she had ever seen it.

'Was that why you made sure that you used contraception with me?' she asked uncertainly. 'Because you were worried that I was going to try and get pregnant by you, to try and trap you, as Patti had done?'

He gave her a very square look. 'Darling,' he said softly, 'wearing a condom that night was the most difficult thing I've ever had to do. I knew a very base desire not to have any kind of barrier between us but to spill my seed into you, to put it very bluntly. I would have been delighted to make you pregnant, but I couldn't trap *you* like that.' And as he bent his head to kiss her again the last remnants of fight went out of her.

Several distracting minutes later, Daisy lifted her head to say, 'It wasn't a very wise thing to do, was it? Asking me to share your apartment so that you could make sure I studied?'

'It was the craziest thing in the world to do,' he agreed. 'But it's amazing how much a man can fool himself when he's deeply in love, and I managed to convince myself that it was the most sensible solution. I only came to England to convince myself that falling for you had been an illusion and it took about two seconds in your company to realise that it was very definitely real.

'When the opportunity came up for me to lure you to my flat in London, I argued with myself that I was only acting in your best interests—which was, of course, self-deception at its highest. But I was determined that our relationship should remain strictly platonic while you were under my care.

'What *that* meant, in fact, was that I subjected myself to a lot of sleepless nights, and a hell of a lot of cold showers.' He paused, and his eyes were soft. 'Until that night when we made love.' He sighed, and bent his head to kiss her shoulder. 'I'd so nearly kept to all my honourable intentions until that incredible night when, in your virginal inno-cence, you managed to display more sensual charm than the world's most accomplished courtesan.'

Her eyes sparkled. 'Are you trying to tell me that I was good in bed?'

He laughed. 'You were superb. But too much of a temptation. Because after we'd made love I knew that if I hung around we'd be married within the month. I had to be sure that was what *you* wanted too. You needed time to spread your wings and live a little. Show what you could do. A man and child is a lot to take on board, you know. Are you sure you want that, sugar?'

Her smile was very complacent. 'You know damned well I'm sure,' she whispered.

His hand slid down to her breast and Daisy shivered with pleasure. 'Can we lock the door?' he whispered. 'Because I can think of several things I'd rather be doing now than talking.'

'Certainly not,' answered Daisy primly as she firmly removed his hand. 'We still haven't dis-cussed the future. What if I told you that I love my job so much that I never, *ever* want to give it up?'

'That's fine by me,' he said equably.

Daisy blinked. Then she thought of something to *really* shock him! 'Or if I said that I hate my job and want you to keep me in your kitchen, barefoot and pregnant?'

There was an answering spark in his eyes. 'That's fine too, sugar. Whatever you want you can have...'

His voice became husky as he began to unbutton her silk jacket to expose the lacy bit of nonsense beneath which made tantalisingly erotic mounds of her breasts. 'So,' he said throatily. 'Shall we make love?'

'I'm not letting you off that easily, Matt Hamilton. You'll have to make a decent woman of me first.'

His face was a picture. 'Oh, hell,' he groaned, in mock despair. 'You're not going to make me wait until we're married, are you?'

Daisy's mouth twitched in amusement. 'Well, if you believe *that*, then you're a bigger fool than I thought!'

'But that's just the trouble,' he admitted ruefully. 'I *am* a fool where you're concerned. You twist me round your little finger—as both our mothers took great delight in reminding me last night when I informed them that I was going to marry you.'

'You *told* them?' Daisy squeaked indignantly. 'Without even asking *me* first? How did you know I hadn't already agreed to marry someone else?'

He gave a crooked smile. 'Well, I knew from my mother that there was no other man in your life. I've kept pretty close tabs on you.'

'And what if there had been?'

'Then I would have been over on the next plane to claim you for myself,' he said masterfully, and Daisy sighed with delight as he kissed her again.

'And were our mothers pleased?' she asked presently.

'Ecstatic. But unsurprised.'

'What if I'd fallen out of love with you in the meantime?'

He shook his head. 'I knew you wouldn't have. Because once you love, Daisy, you love for ever. Like me.' He lifted the neat French plait and twisted it between his fingers. 'Do you still wear your hair loose?'

'Only in bed.'

His eyes glittered. 'I'd like to see it.'

'I'm sure you will,' she murmured against his cheek, then suddenly pulled herself out of his arms.

He gave a sigh as she walked towards the door. 'I want to make love to you,' he murmured. 'But I guess I can wait until tonight when we've put Sophie to bed. Daisy, what *are* you doing?'

Daisy locked the door, pocketed the key, marched firmly over to her desk, where she said crisply into the intercom, 'Hold all my calls, please!' then turned demurely to face him. 'Matt?'

'What?'

'You know those macho-man qualities you teased me about earlier?'

'I do.'

'Well,' she said, slightly breathlessly because her heart was pounding so erratically, 'I think I might be quite old-fashioned at heart after all...'

'And?'

'I think I might rather like them. So if you *were* planning to have your wicked way with me—' she sighed in an exaggerated fashion '—then I guess there would be nothing I could do to stop you— Matt! *Matt?*' This as she sank onto the soft carpet with one very aroused man on top of her. 'What do you think you're doing?'

He deftly unclipped her bra and gave her the most delectably wolfish smile as he lowered his head towards her breasts. 'I'm going to ravish you, Miss Blair, so you'd better just lie back and enjoy it.'

And making mad, passionate love with Matt on the office floor sure beat the weekly 'ideas' meeting, was Daisy's last, fleetingly logical thought . . .

'So the Prince put the glass slipper onto Cinderella's foot and it fitted perfectly, and then he realised that *she* was the girl he had fallen so madly in love with at the ball.' Daisy dropped a gentle kiss onto the top of Sophie's sleepy head.

'What happened den?' squeaked Sophie, who had heard the story at least a hundred times.

'Why, the Prince asked Cinderella to marry him, and they both lived happily ever after,' said Daisy triumphantly.

'Like you and Daddy?'

Daisy met an amused pair of grey eyes over the top of their daughter's head, and nodded. 'Just like me and Daddy,' she agreed quickly, but she had to swallow the lump of happiness which had momentarily constricted her throat.

Sophie batted her grey eyes unashamedly at her doting father. 'Now Daddy tell it!' she demanded.

Daisy could see Matt wavering. He was like putty in his daughter's hand. And in hers, she thought with loving satisfaction. 'Not tonight, darling,' she said.

'But Mum-*ah*!'

'Because we're going to the seaside tomorrow,' Daisy reminded her softly. 'And you need lots of sleep to build all those sandcastles, don't you?'

'Mm,' agreed Sophie, snuggling down, thumb firmly in place in her mouth, already almost half-asleep. 'Kiss, please!'

Matt bent his head to kiss his daughter, and then Daisy did the same.

'Night, night!' mumbled Sophie sleepily.

'Night, night,' they echoed in unison, then Daisy switched on the nightlight and they quietly left the room.

Hand in hand they wandered into the sitting room. Before them the London skyline twinkled more brightly than the Milky Way, and Daisy sighed with pleasure as Matt took her into his arms and looked down at her with tender eyes.

'Hungry?' he asked.

'Not particularly.'

'Tired, then?'

She shook her head. 'Not a bit.'

He gave a mock sigh. 'Shame.'

'Oh?' she queried innocently. 'Why's that?'

'I was going to suggest an early night...'

'You know I'm always open to suggestions,' she whispered against his lips, and he pulled her tightly into his arms...

She must have fallen asleep after he'd made love to her, because when she opened her eyes it was to find Matt propped up on one elbow, studying her face intently. His broad chest was bare and faintly sweat-sheened, and only one rumpled corner of the sheet prevented him from being completely naked, and Daisy felt the warm, tightening rush of that oh, so familiar sensation. She was aroused. *Again.* And so soon!

He smiled lazily. He'd noticed, of course. Matt noticed everything. But he didn't start to make love to her immediately, as he usually would have done.

Instead he picked her left hand up, kissed the palm, and idly began to turn the shiny band of gold which encircled her ring finger.

'So do *you* believe in fairy stories?' he asked suddenly.

Daisy smiled. 'Sophie does.'

'But do you?' he persisted.

'You know I do,' she whispered huskily. 'And you?'

'Aren't I too old?' he teased sardonically.

'Matt!'

He smiled at the question he read in her eyes. 'A year of marriage to you has been little short of heaven. For me and for Sophie.' He frowned. 'Except that lately there's something you're not telling me.'

Daisy's heart pounded. 'Meaning?'

He gave a light shrug. 'Little things. These past weeks you've grown less kittenish. There's something different in your eyes, in the way you smile...'

'You've guessed?' she hazarded tremulously.

'You're pregnant, aren't you, sugar?'

The unashamed joy in his voice made it impossible for her to do little more than nod, and her cheeks were wet against his bare shoulder as he gathered her into his warm embrace.

They stayed there, silently holding one another for a little while, and then Matt smiled into her hair.

'Do you know something, Daisy, darling?' he murmured as he began to slide his hand deliciously over her breast. 'I really think I *do* believe in fairy tales after all.'

Coming Next Month

HARLEQUIN PRESENTS®

THE BEST HAS JUST GOTTEN BETTER!

#1929 A MARRIAGE TO REMEMBER Carole Mortimer
Three years ago Adam Carmichael had walked out on Maggi—now he was back! Divorce seemed the only way to get him out of her life for good. But Adam wasn't going to let her go without a fight!

#1930 RED-HOT AND RECKLESS Miranda Lee
(Scandals!)
Ben Sinclair just couldn't put his schoolboy obsession with Amber behind him. She *still* thought she could have anything because she was rich and beautiful. But now Ben had a chance to get even with her at last....

#1931 TIGER, TIGER Robyn Donald
Leo Dacre was determined to find out what had happened to his runaway half brother, but Tansy was just as determined not to tell him! It was a clash of equals...so who would be the winner?

#1932 FLETCHER'S BABY Anne McAllister
Sam Fletcher never ran away from difficult situations, so when Josie revealed that she was expecting his child, marriage seemed the practical solution. And he wasn't going to take no for an answer!

#1933 THE SECRET MOTHER Lee Wilkinson
(Nanny Wanted!)
Caroline had promised herself that one day she would be back for Caitlin. Now, four years later, she's applying for the job of her nanny. Matthew Carran, the interviewer, doesn't *seem* to recognize her. But he has a hidden agenda....

#1934 HUSBAND BY CONTRACT Helen Brooks
(Husbands and Wives)
For Donato Vittoria, marriage was a lifetime commitment. Or so Grace had thought—until she'd discovered his betrayal, and fled. But in Donato's eyes he was still her husband, and he wanted her back in his life—and in his bed!

Take 4 bestselling love stories FREE

Plus get a FREE surprise gift!

Special Limited-time Offer

Mail to Harlequin Reader Service®

3010 Walden Avenue
P.O. Box 1867
Buffalo, N.Y. 14240-1867

YES! Please send me 4 free Harlequin Presents® novels and my free surprise gift. Then send me 6 brand-new novels every month, which I will receive months before they appear in bookstores. Bill me at the low price of $2.90 each plus 25¢ delivery and applicable sales tax, if any*. That's the complete price and a savings of over 10% off the cover prices—quite a bargain! I understand that accepting the books and gift places me under no obligation ever to buy any books. I can always return a shipment and cancel at any time. Even if I never buy another book from Harlequin, the 4 free books and the surprise gift are mine to keep forever.

106 BPA A3UL

Name	(PLEASE PRINT)
Address	Apt. No.
City	State	Zip

This offer is limited to one order per household and not valid to present Harlequin Presents® subscribers. *Terms and prices are subject to change without notice. Sales tax applicable in N.Y.

Free Gift Offer

As Seen on TV!

With a Free Gift proof-of-purchase
from any Harlequin® book, you can receive
a beautiful cubic zirconia pendant.

This stunning marquise-shaped stone is a genuine cubic
zirconia—accented by an 18" gold tone necklace.
(Approximate retail value $19.95)

Send for yours today...
compliments of ◈HARLEQUIN®

To receive your free gift, a cubic zirconia pendant, send us one original proof-of-purchase, photocopies not accepted, from the back of any Harlequin Romance®, Harlequin Presents®, Harlequin Temptation®, Harlequin Superromance®, Harlequin Intrigue®, Harlequin American Romance®, or Harlequin Historicals® title available at your favorite retail outlet, together with the Free Gift Certificate, plus a check or money order for $1.65 U.S./$2.15 CAN. (do not send cash) to cover postage and handling, payable to Harlequin Free Gift Offer. We will send you the specified gift. Allow 6 to 8 weeks for delivery. Offer good until December 31, 1997, or while quantities last. Offer valid in the U.S. and Canada only.

Free Gift Certificate

Name: _____

Address: _____

City: _____ State/Province: _____ Zip/Postal Code: _____

Mail this certificate, one proof-of-purchase and a check or money order for postage and handling to: HARLEQUIN FREE GIFT OFFER 1997. In the U.S.: 3010 Walden Avenue, P.O. Box 9071, Buffalo NY 14269-9057. In Canada: P.O. Box 604, Fort Erie, Ontario L2Z 5X3.

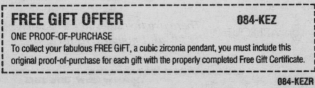

FREE GIFT OFFER   084-KEZ

ONE PROOF-OF-PURCHASE
To collect your fabulous FREE GIFT, a cubic zirconia pendant, you must include this
original proof-of-purchase for each gift with the properly completed Free Gift Certificate.

084-KEZR